The Miseducation of Power:

A Tale of Privilege, Corruption, and Control

Kevin Joynt

Disclaimer:

This is a work of fiction. All names, characters, places, organizations, and events are products of the author's imagination or are used fictitiously. Any resemblance to actual persons, living or dead, or to real institutions or events is entirely coincidental.

While the narrative may be informed by broad themes familiar to public life—such as power, influence, and institutional culture—it is presented through wholly fictional constructs. Characterizations and events have been shaped with creative intent and are not drawn from, nor intended to represent, any specific individual or real-world occurrence.

Cover design by Kevin Joynt
ISBN (Paperback): 979-8-9897937-2-3
ISBN (eBook): 979-8-9897937-3-0
First Edition
Printed in the United States of America

*This book is dedicated to my lovely wife.
You deserved better!*

Table of Contents

Chapter 1: Hospital Room, April 1, 1962

Dawn bled through the white walls of St. Elizabeth's Hospital, casting an almost holy light on the narrow bed where Sue Pollock lay, pale and motionless. The scent of antiseptics clung thick in the air, but her senses barely registered it. Hours of grueling labor had wrung her thin frame dry, leaving only a hollow exhaustion behind. Sedatives dulled her pain, but they also obscured the world around her, shrouding it in a fog she drifted through, barely aware of the distant voices or the gentle shuffle of nurses in the room. Her mind stretched back to the pain that had racked her body earlier, a violent and humbling ordeal that had left her emptied and yearning for comfort.

Somewhere nearby, a nurse held her son, Anthony. They weighed him, measured his tiny limbs, scrubbed his skin, performing their duties with mechanical precision. Sue had scarcely seen him since his arrival. She had heard his first cry faintly through her clouded senses, but that primal bond, the sudden rush of maternal affection she had expected, was elusive, slipping further as she floated deeper into a sedative-induced calm.

The door creaked open, and Barton Pollock entered, cutting a sharp figure against the backdrop of sterile walls. Even here, in the harsh light of the hospital, his suit was immaculate, his posture unshaken. Men like him didn't enter delivery rooms. They waited in private lounges, sipping coffee and glancing at their watches, treating childbirth as another inevitable hurdle to observe from a distance. Barton had spent those hours down the hall, engrossed in a business magazine, his duty only requiring a brief appearance.

He moved toward her with controlled steps, his face betraying not even a flicker of emotion. He stood over her like a statue, an emblem of strength without warmth. Reaching out, he touched her shoulder lightly. "Well done," he said, his voice soft but hollow. It was the kind of praise one might give a business associate for finalizing a difficult deal. "You did it."

Sue's lips parted, a faint sound escaping, but her words tangled in the fog of sedatives and her own disappointment. She blinked, struggling to focus on him, her husband, the man she had once thought would protect and cherish her. She had hoped, despite herself, for a moment of warmth, of real connection. But even here, with their newborn son nearby, she saw only the familiar indifference in his eyes.

Barton's hand rested a moment longer, and then he pulled back, his gaze drifting to the door. "The doctors will take care of you now," he said, straightening. "I'll leave you to rest." The congratulations had been given, the formality observed. He had fulfilled his role, and now, he was free to return to his world, far from the mess and blood of childbirth.

The door closed softly behind him, and Sue's heart sank as the room grew still. She drifted deeper into the haze, the sedatives thickening around her thoughts like a heavy blanket. A subtle warmth bloomed within her, a strange, almost comforting numbness, unlike anything she had felt before. This void, this tranquil state—it shielded her, made the loneliness bearable. In that moment, she welcomed it, clutching the sensation like a secret.

Her solitude was interrupted as the door opened once more, and a nurse entered, moving with brisk efficiency, her uniform crisp against the muted hospital light. She glanced at Sue, her tone professional but distant. "How are you feeling, Mrs. Pollock?" she asked, already reaching for Sue's chart.

"Tired," Sue replied, her voice a thin whisper. The exhaustion seemed to weigh down every word, as though speaking itself was a burden. She barely heard herself, lost as she was in the growing blur around her.

The nurse nodded, barely acknowledging her as she adjusted the IV, tapping a syringe thoughtfully. "The doctor ordered something for the pain," she said, filling the syringe with practiced ease. "A mild sedative. It'll help you rest." She injected the clear liquid into Sue's IV line, watching as Sue's eyes began to flutter, her eyelids growing heavier as the warmth of drugs coursed through her veins.

Sue's world zoomed out as the room seemed to float away, leaving only the soothing warmth that pulled her further from reality. It was like nothing she had ever known—so safe, so quiet, and far better than the chill of her husband's detachment or the ache of her self-doubt. Her mind drifted, slipping from thought to thought, barely tethered to her surroundings. She no longer cared about the baby, about Barton, or anything beyond this blissful calm.

The doctor entered briefly, exchanging words with the nurse in low tones, as though Sue was no longer present. He glanced at her still form, then murmured, "Keep her on the barbiturates for the next few days. She needs to rest."

And with that, they left her again, floating in her sea of numbness. For the first time in years, she felt a strange sense of relief, a release from the constant pressure to perform, to be something more than what she felt inside. This warmth, this freedom from her own life, was a comfort she hadn't realized she needed. In the haze of that April morning, with her son somewhere nearby and her husband's hollow words still lingering in the air, Sue Pollock found her first taste of oblivion. And as the drugs pulled her deeper, she welcomed it, letting the darkness close around her.

It was only supposed to be temporary, an aid to help her recover from childbirth, but Sue clung to that numbing calm with a hunger that surprised even her. The world had receded, leaving her cocooned in warmth, sheltered from Barton's cold disinterest, from the hollow title of "mother" she felt unworthy of. In those fleeting hours, she found herself fearing only one thing: the moment she would wake up, forced to return to the unforgiving light of her life.

Chapter 2: The Long Road to Springfield

The 1959 Chevy Impala rumbled down the highway, its engine, a steady background hum beneath the whirlwind in Jarod Davis's mind. The early spring sun was dipping lower now, casting a golden light across the passing fields, but Jarod barely noticed. He was stuck somewhere between dread and anticipation, staring straight ahead as the miles rolled by. They were heading to Springfield, Massachusetts, to meet their first grandchild. It should have been a joyous moment, but for Jarod, it was clouded by a nagging sense of unease that had been growing since they left Detroit.

Natalie sat beside him, her posture relaxed, though she hadn't turned a page in the magazine that was resting on her lap for at least thirty minutes. She wasn't one to miss the subtle shifts in Jarod's mood. His jaw was clenched, and his fingers were gripping the steering wheel a little too hard. She could practically feel the weight of his thoughts pressing down on the space between them. But what pulled her out of her quiet contemplation, was the sudden burst of static from the radio, followed by a fragment of a song, then more static, then a preacher's booming voice, then static again.

Jarod's hand was on the dial, twisting it back and forth with the precision of a man who had no idea what he was looking for. The radio spat out snippets of sound—a guitar riff here, a news anchor's monotone there—before dissolving into a hiss of white noise. He frowned, leaning closer to the dashboard as if proximity might magically clarify the signal.

"Jarod," Natalie said, with a voice sharp enough to cut through the chaos. "For heaven's sake, pick a station and leave it alone. I'd like to listen to something that doesn't sound like a cat walking on a piano."

Jarod froze with his fingers hovering around the dial. He glanced at her, sheepish but defiant. "I'm just trying to find something good. Everything out here is either gospel or static. You'd think in 1962 we'd have better reception."

"You've been at it for twenty minutes," Natalie shot back in a dry tone. "If I hear one more second of that preacher yelling about sin, I'm going to throw this magazine at your head."

Jarod chuckled, but his hand didn't leave the dial. He gave it another twist, and the radio landed on a faint, crackling version of "Dream Lover" by Bobby Darin. He paused and tilted his head as if considering it, but the signal wavered, and the song slipped back into static. He groaned then slapped the dashboard lightly. "See? This is impossible. It's like the universe doesn't want us to have music."

Natalie let out a long and exaggerated sigh, then reached over as if to smack his hand away from the dial. "Enough. If you can't find something, turn it off. I'd rather sit in silence than listen to you torture that poor radio."

Jarod hesitated, his hand still hovering, but then he relented and pulled it back. The car was suddenly quiet except for the hum of the engine and the faint whistle of wind through the cracked window. He drummed his fingers on the steering wheel, but the rhythm was restless and uneven. "Fine," he muttered. "But don't blame me if you get bored."

"I'd rather be bored than annoyed," Natalie said, though her lips twitched with the hint of a smile. She set the magazine aside and turned to look at him, her gaze steady. "You're not fooling me. This isn't about the radio. What's really eating at you?"

Jarod just stared straight ahead, his eyes fixed on the road. For a moment, he didn't answer. Then he sighed, a deep and heavy sound that seemed to carry the weight of all his unspoken worries. "It's just him," he finally said. "I just... I don't know how I'm going to visit with that man without saying something I'll regret."

Natalie didn't need to ask who 'that man' was. Barton Pollock, their son-in-law. A man born into wealth and privilege. A man who carried his family's name like a badge of superiority. Barton was the last in a line of Pollocks who had grown rich off the buggy whip industry. It's a fact that Jarod found laughable, given how long ago that industry had been relevant. But what irritated Jarod most was Barton's arrogance, his absolute certainty that wealth alone made him better than everyone else.

"Jarod," Natalie said, in a soft but still firm voice. "Pull yourself together. You're too old to let this get under your skin. Besides, this isn't about Barton, it's about Sue and her baby. Don't let him ruin it."

Jarod nodded but didn't loosen his grip on the steering wheel. "You're right. It's just... where did you go wrong with Sue?" As he cleverly responded, the corners of his mouth twitched upward as if trying to soften the blow of his words.

Natalie gave him a look, half affection, half warning. "You hold your tongue. Of all the stupid things to say about your daughter, that's one that you shall never repeat. She's beautiful, strong, and kind... despite your genetic contribution."

Jarod grinned; the banter games were on. They had always used it to lighten the load, and he couldn't resist pushing it just a little further. "I'm not that old," he said with a mischievous glint in his eye. "Besides, I look younger than your sister Beth."

Natalie's face shifted, just for a moment, before she fired back. "Yeah, right. Iron out those wrinkles and dye the gray out of your hair, and you might have a shot, but leave Beth out of it.

Jarod knew better than to press his luck further. He had hit a nerve, and it wasn't one he intended to hit hard. Beth, with her ageless beauty and effortless charm, had always been a sore spot for Natalie, and Jarod could see that, even after all these years, it still stung.

"Agh," Jarod sighed, leaning back into the seat as if trying to sink into it. "It's just Barton. He has no real substance, you know? He's all show. He's never worked a day in his life. He's so self-absorbed. I don't even believe he knows how to love anyone but himself."

Natalie gave a half-nod as her lips pursed thoughtfully. "Maybe, but you must remember, Sue didn't just marry Barton. She married the security and the lifestyle that comes with him. How many nights did we sit up wondering how we were going to pay for things, how would we survive? Sue remembers that, and now, she doesn't have the burden of those worries."

Jarod grunted. Natalie always had a way of seeing the bigger picture, the pieces he didn't want to admit were there. He thought back to when he first meet Barton. He was charming enough, with that smooth smile and firm handshake, but Jarod saw through it. There was a hollowness to the man, something untrustworthy that made Jarod's stomach turn every time Barton opened his mouth.

"Yeah," Jarod muttered. "But he doesn't love her."

Natalie didn't respond right away. Instead, she reached over and patted Jarod's arm with her warm and steady hand. "Maybe he doesn't love her the way you think a man should love his wife... but Jarod, Sue made her choice. We have two options: we can let it go and be in her life, be in our grandkid's life. Or we can fight it and lose them. I'd rather be there for them."

Jarod stared at the road ahead, allowing the weight of her words settle in. He knew she was spot-on. Natalie was always better at navigating difficult people. Barton was the gatekeeper to their daughter's life now, and no matter how much Jarod despised the man, he wasn't willing to risk losing Sue or their grandchild over it.

"I always stand with you," Jarod said quietly, his voice tinged with reluctance. "But I just hope Barton behaves himself. I can't stand the idea of tiptoeing around that jackass."

Natalie smiled with her hand still resting on his arm. "Then don't tiptoe. Show him you're happy to see him. Congratulate him. But for God's sake, don't go in there expecting trouble. If you do, that's all you'll find."

For the first time since they'd set out on this drive, Jarod felt a sliver of relief. He glanced over at Natalie, the wife he'd shared his life with for all these years, and the tension waned just a little. She was right, as she always was. He needed to let this go, for Sue's sake, for his own.

The road ahead still stretched long and uncertain, but in that moment, with Natalie's hand on his arm and the Impala humming beneath them, Jarod allowed himself a flicker of hope. Maybe, just maybe, this visit wouldn't be so bad after all.

Chapter 3: The Red Car and the Baby

The Pollock estate loomed ahead, a grand and gated home that made it perfectly clear the uninvited poor would be dealt with to the fullest extent the law allowed.

Their Chevy Impala made its way up the winding driveway, the gravel crunching under the tires. The scent of fresh spring air, damp earth, and budding leaves filled the air, yet the atmosphere inside the car wasn't fresh.

Jarod, still gripping the steering wheel with calloused hands from years on the assembly line, let out a slow breath as the mansion came into full view. Its grandeur was undeniable. It was an imposing structure with white columns that could support the very weight of the sky. This was a house built on old money that had shaped America's upper class long before the war, before the rise of the unions, and long before the working-class had any say in their own fate.

Beside him, Natalie adjusted her purse in her lap, her eyes bright with the anticipation of seeing their daughter and meeting their first grandchild. "Jarod, leave the bags in the car," she said, her voice betraying the anticipation she felt. "We'll come back for them after we see the baby."

Jarod nodded with a fixed gaze at the mansion. "Sure, sure," he replied, though his thoughts were elsewhere. He was thinking about Sue, about the girl she used to be, before she had married into this world of privilege and socialites, before the mansion and the marble floors, before Barton Pollock. He shifted the car into park, the engine's rumble fading into the quiet of the estate as he killed the ignition.

Natalie was already halfway out of the car, her excitement palpable. "I'm hot on your tail, my darling," Jarod called after her, managing a smile despite his worry. He barely had time to close his door before Natalie was at the front steps, her shoes tapping lightly against the stone as she hurried to the massive front doors.

Inside, Sue Pollock had been pacing the length of the foyer with frayed nerves despite the tranquil setting. The polished marble floor reflected the ornate chandelier above which casted an intricate pattern of light across the room, but Sue hardly noticed. She was watching the clock, counting down the minutes until her parents arrived. This was their first visit since Anthony was born, and while she longed to see them, a part of her dreaded their arrival. How could they possibly understand the world she now inhabited? How could they reconcile the love and warmth inside their modest Detroit home with the cold grandeur of the Pollock estate?

The sound of a car rolling up brought her to the window. Her heart leapt as she saw the familiar Impala pull up. She took a deep breath, smoothed her dress, and plastered on a smile that she hoped would hide the cracks in her carefully constructed life. The doorbell rang, and she hurried to open it with her smile faltering only slightly as she took in the sight of her parents standing on the threshold.

"Dad, Mom, oh it's so good to see you! Come in, come in!" Sue's voice was bright as she ushered them inside. The entry way seemed even larger with the three of them standing there, the ceiling stretching high above them like a cathedral. Jarod took it all in with a slow sweep of his eyes while noting the cold and hard edges of the room: the polished floor, the gold accents, the massive staircase that spiraled upwards as if it were trying to escape the weight of the past.

"Honey, I love you, but where's that baby?" Natalie's voice cut through the stillness while her eyes darted around in search of her grandchild. Her excitement was almost desperate, as if the sight of him would somehow dispel the unease that had settled in her heart the moment they pulled up to the estate.

"Wait, wait, wait," Jarod interjected while stepping forward to wrap Sue in a tight embrace. "First, I want a hug from my baby. A quick one. Then it's off to see your newborn." His voice was gruff, but the emotion behind it was unmistakable. He held Sue for a moment longer than necessary, as if trying to anchor her to the memory of who she used to be, his little girl, the one who had always been so full of life, so full of dreams.

Natalie joined in by wrapping her arms around them both in a group hug. "Now let's go see our grandbaby," she said as her voice strained with emotion. For this brief moment Sue felt a reminder of her family's love and warmth that had always been their foundation. But, as they pulled away, the coldness of the mansion seeped back in and chilled the moment into a fragile memory.

Sue led them upstairs with her footsteps growing softer as they approached the nursery. "Anthony's looking forward to meeting you," she whispered, her voice catching slightly as she pushed open the door. "I've been telling him all about you, but let's keep it down. He's taking a nap."

The nursery was a stark contrast to the house's grandness. Pale blue walls, a white crib draped in soft lace, and shelves filled with plush toys that looked expensive yet eager to be touched by small hands. It was a room designed to portray love. As Jarod stepped in, his inhibitions melted away.

Natalie's eyes filled with tears as she gazed at the tiny bundle in the crib. "He's so beautiful, Sue," she whispered as her voice again trembled with emotion. She reached out, hesitated for a moment, then gently touched the baby's cheek. Anthony stirred but didn't wake. His small face scrunching up as if the very act of existing was an effort.

Sue awkwardly smiled. It just dawned on her that she clearly didn't feel as strong a connection to her own newborn son as her mother does; a woman who was a complete stranger to her child until a few moments ago. Sue didn't want to face this reality, at least not right now, so she chose to change direction. "He's perfect, isn't he? Um, let's leave him to sleep and go to the kitchen. I'm sure you must be hungry and thirsty after your long drive."

They left the nursery as quietly as they had entered while making their way down the grand staircase and into a kitchen that looked more like a set from a magazine than a place where meals were actually prepared. The counters gleamed under the soft lighting and everything was in its place, with untouched perfection.

"Here we are," Sue said, gesturing to the spread of food on the counter. "We have fondue, onion dip, and shrimp cocktails. These are the hors d'oeuvres of the day. It's what's served at all the best galas"... and they just so happen to be Sue's favorites. "If you'd like, I can mix up some drinks. You know, Manhattans... or whatever. Barton says I make a choice cocktail. Me, I'm going to have a julep. What'll you have?"

"Oh, thank you, darling. It's so good to see you! But, I think I'd prefer something that will quench my thirst after such a long drive, like some iced tea or lemonade if you have it. Really, anything without alcohol," Natalie replied with a soft yet resolute voice. She had never been one for drinking and the sight of Sue so eager to mix a cocktail, especially with a newborn in the house, set off warning bells in her mind. However, she kept her concerns to herself, not wanting to spoil the reunion.

Jarod, who had been watching Sue closely, nodded in agreement. "I'll have whatever you're having dear," he said, his spirit light but his eyes heavy with worry. He wasn't much of a drinker either, but he'd do anything to connect with his daughter, to reach across the growing chasm that separated them. He knew that drinkers preferred the company of other drinkers, and if that was what it took to get through to Sue, then he'd nurse a julep all night.

Before Sue could respond, the sound of custom shoes on the tile floor announced Barton Pollock's arrival. He entered the kitchen with the kind of presence that demanded attention, tall, lean, and impeccably dressed, his tailored suit fitting him like a second skin. His smile was tight, almost predatory, as he surveyed the room. "That's a beautiful red car parked in the courtyard." Barton's voice was smooth, almost casual, but the words carried an undercurrent that Jarod couldn't ignore. "How was your drive?"

Jarod's posture slightly slumped, catching the insinuation immediately. Barton wasn't referring to the color of the Impala; he was making a pointed remark about its origins. Barton saw unions as no different from communism, and Jarod, a proud union man, knew exactly what Barton was implying, but he forced a smile and said, "The drive was great. It only took us about eight hours on the new interstate. Congratulations on becoming a father; you must be thrilled."

Barton's smile widened, though it didn't reach his eyes. "Ha, thrilled, yes indeed," he replied, his tone laced with sarcasm. "Sue, darling, I've brought your medication."

Jarod's heart sank as he watched Barton hand Sue a small bottle of pills. Sue's face lit up as she quickly unscrewed the cap, shaking one out and swallowing it down with the last of her julep. "Looks like I need another drink," she said with a laugh that made Jarod's blood run cold.

"What are those?" Jarod asked, the words escaping his mouth before he could stop them. His concern was raw and unfiltered, as he stared at the bottle in Sue's hand.

Barton didn't miss a beat. "That is Sue's bitch pill, as we call them," he said, his voice dripping with disdain. "The doctors call them bar-bitch-urates, but we like calling them bitch pills. They're for her postpartum depression and bar her from turning into, well, a bitch."

For a moment, the room seemed to freeze. Natalie's eyes widened in shock while her mouth opened slightly with a mix of disbelief and concern. Jarod, on the other hand, felt a surge of anger rising from deep within. A slow burn that ignited memories of battles fought, both on the warfront and in the union halls back in Detroit. He had faced down men who thought they were better than him before, but none had ever insulted his family like this.

Before Jarod could respond, Natalie, always the diplomat, stepped in. "Before you make that next drink Sue, would you mind showing me around and telling me what you've been up to? Let's go have a look." Her voice was calm but the urgency in her eyes was unmistakable. She was trying to divert the conversation and pull her daughter away from whatever toxic influence Barton had over her. Natalie knew that now was not the time for confrontation, especially not with her vulnerable daughter standing in the middle.

Sue brightened at the suggestion, a fleeting relief crossing her features. "Oh yes, come see my craft room. It's divine," she said with a bit too enthusiastic voice. It was as if she were trying to convince herself as much as her mother.

As Sue and Natalie left the kitchen, Jarod found himself alone with Barton. The silence that settled between them was thick and oppressive. Barton moved to a sideboard and casually poured himself a drink, his movements deliberate and calculated. He took a sip and then turned towards Jarod while leaning against the counter. He regarded Jarod with a look that was equal parts disdain and curiosity.

"Jarod, why don't we take a stroll to my study? Follow me." Barton said, his tone devoid of the warmth that should accompany an invitation. It wasn't a suggestion; it was more a command.

Jarod knew that refusing would only escalate the tension, so he nodded curtly and followed Barton down the hallway. The study was a dark room filled with heavily polished wood and the scent of leather-bound books. A fire crackled in the large stone fireplace that cast flickering shadows across the walls adorned with portraits of long-dead Pollocks with cold and judging eyes. Jarod could feel them watching. Their presence was a reminder that he's a guest here in a world where he didn't belong.

Barton moved to the window and stared at the Impala parked in the courtyard. "Yes, that sure is a nice-looking red car you have," he said, the smirk returning to his lips.

Jarod had enough. He squared his shoulders and turned his gaze steady towards Barton. "Are you referring to the color, or are you insinuating it's some sort of communist car?"

Barton turned slowly, clearly enjoying the game. "It was built by union workers, right? That is basically communism."

Jarod's fists clenched at his sides, but he kept his voice even. "I belong to a union and can assure you that I am not a communist. I work for a privately owned corporation. Chevrolet is in no way owned by the government. The union is an organized group of workers banded together to maximize our earning power. The government does not have a seat at the table. There is nothing remotely communist about that car or what we do to build them."

Barton's smirk faltered, if only for a moment. He hadn't expected Jarod to push back so directly, and it unsettled him. But Barton was not one to back down easily. "I suppose you believe FDR's New Deal isn't a communist push either," he said, his voice dripping with condescension.

Jarod took a deep breath, steadying himself. He had seen Barton's type before, men who believed their wealth and status gave them the right to look down on others, to manipulate and control. But Jarod had fought too hard for too long to let someone like Barton get under his skin.

"The U.S. has implemented some social welfare programs and regulations over the years, but these do not make the country socialist, let alone communist," Jarod said, his voice measured. "Instead, these programs represent a mixed economy, where some elements of government intervention exist alongside a predominantly capitalist system. Taxes are collected to pay living wages to employees who conduct services we need, services that private industry has little incentive to provide. Moreover, these living wages put pressure on private industry to pay living wages or risk losing their best employees to the government sector. Since the New Deal has been in place, the middle class has grown substantially and has become the lifeblood of our thriving economy. The New Deal is an investment in our country, and we should take pride in what we can accomplish together and the security it provides."

Barton's expression darkened. He wasn't used to being challenged in his own home, especially not by someone he considered beneath him. "If you say so," Barton replied, his tone icy. "Just know, you are putting your daughter and grandson in financial peril. My inheritance can only go so far with our current tax codes. What are we to do? When my grandpa built the family fortune, the working class knew their place, and so did the government. Now, my money is being taken, my future is put in jeopardy, so the working class can have...stuff. It's robbery, pure and simple."

Jarod felt his patience wearing thin. He had worked too hard, sacrificed too much, to listen to this spoiled man whine about paying his fair share. "We live in a country without royalty, where hard work and determination dictate wealth, not the family someone was born into," Jarod said, his voice firm. "You can work too. You're well educated, you can get a job to support your family, earn a good income. You already have a nice home. You are in an advantageous spot and aren't a victim."

Barton's eyes narrowed, his face flushing with anger. "Never. I will never work for someone. It is appalling to suggest I should. Not only am I not a worker, but I am not interested in business hours. I don't have time for that. But, if things don't change, your grandson will probably have to walk that path, and what a shame that will be."

The words hung heavy and final. Jarod could see that this conversation was going nowhere and, frankly, he supported the idea of his grandson having a career. Barton was entrenched in his beliefs though, his mind closed off to any perspective that didn't align with his own privileged worldview. Jarod knew there was no reasoning with a man like Barton, and continuing to try would only lead to more conflict.

Jarod took a step back, his posture relaxing slightly as he forced a smile. "Well, why don't we go see what the girls are up to," he suggested, hoping to steer the conversation away from the brewing storm.

Barton waved a hand dismissively, turning his attention back to the window. "Go ahead. I'll be down shortly," he said, his voice void of any real interest.

Jarod didn't need to be told twice. He turned and left the study, his footsteps echoing down the hallway as he made his way back through the mansion. The knot in his chest had loosened but the unease remained. He couldn't shake the feeling that something was terribly wrong, that the life Sue had chosen would slowly unravel her.

As he approached the craft room, Jarod heard the sound of laughter, Sue's chuckle, but it was wrong, too loud and sloppy. He quickened his pace, turning the corner just in time to see Natalie and Sue standing by a large table cluttered with art supplies. Natalie was smiling, but there was a worry that Jarod recognized all too well.

"Sue, are you OK?" Jarod asked as he entered the room, his voice laced with concern.

Sue turned to him, her eyes glassy and unfocused. "Oh, Dad's here. I'm great, it's so good to see you," she slurred, her words barely coherent. The sight of her hit Jarod like a punch to the gut. This wasn't his daughter, this was someone else, someone lost in intoxication and adrift in a world that didn't care about her well-being.

Just then, a cry pierced the air, Anthony's cry. Sue looked around, confused, as if she couldn't quite place where the sound was coming from.

Natalie faced her daughter with resolve. "Yes, Dad is here too. Why don't you go with Dad to the patio, and I'll get Anthony," she said, her voice calm but firm, taking charge of the situation with the kind of quiet authority that Jarod had always admired in her.

Sue nodded, swaying slightly as Jarod guided her out of the room and towards the patio. The cool evening air washed over them as they stepped outside, but it did little to clear the fog in Sue's mind. She leaned heavily on Jarod, her steps unsteady, her words slurring together as she tried to make sense of the world around her.

Jarod's heart ached as he looked at her, at the daughter he had once known so well but who now seemed like a stranger. "Sue, it's so good to see you, but it's getting late. I think it might be time for bed. Let's get a good night's sleep and then pick back up tomorrow," he said gently, hoping to coax her into resting.

Sue giggled, a high-pitched, almost childlike sound that sent chills down Jarod's spine. "Aw, the party was just getting started. Did you know I have a baby? Don't change his diapers though...Barton only wants me or the nanny to do that. He's worried people might think his weenie is small too," the words tumbling out of her mouth in a garbled mess. It was hard for Jarod to understand where her mind had gone, and so fast, and what she was thinking...and what those pills were doing to her.

Jarod felt a surge of anger and sadness as he listened to her ramble. This wasn't right, none of this was right, but he forced himself to stay calm, to keep his voice steady as he guided her back inside. "Let's get you to bed, sweetheart," he said, his tone gentle yet firm as he led her to her sleeping quarters.

Meanwhile, Natalie had gone to the nursery to find Anthony, only to be met by a woman she hadn't seen before, a nanny. Relief flooded through her as she realized that someone was there to take care of her grandbaby. The nanny smiled politely and said, "I'll prepare Anthony to be seen and bring him out to be adored."

Natalie nodded, her mind racing as she tried to process everything that had happened since her arrival. She couldn't believe what she was seeing, her daughter, the girl she had raised with so much love and care, was now lost in a haze of pills and alcohol, with a husband who seemed more interested in his own status than in the well-being of his family. But there was no time to dwell on it for now. She had to stay strong, for Sue, for Anthony.

A few moments later, Natalie appeared holding a now-awake and cooing Anthony in her arms.

"Here he is Jarod, let's spend the evening with him," her voice was soft and full of warmth. Jarod looked at his grandson, and for the first time since he first set eyes on Sue, a genuine smile spread across his face. He reached out to take the baby, feeling the small weight in his arms. For a moment, all the tension, all the worry, melted away. Anthony gurgled softly, his tiny fingers curling around Jarod's thumb. In this moment, Anthony, for the first time, feels unconditional love, something his life will substantially lack. Natalie, seated beside him, watched with quiet reverence, her fingers lightly brushing Anthony's tiny hand as she whispered sweet words to him.

This was what they had come for, the chance to bond with their grandson, to fill the gaps in their lives that had widened since Sue's marriage.

Sue, meanwhile, had succumbed to the fog of intoxication, her body sprawled out across the plush bed in her room, completely oblivious to the world. The barbiturates and cocktails had worked their numbing magic, pulling her down into a dreamless sleep. The mansion, vast and echoing, held her within its cold walls, while her parents, too far away from her emotionally and physically, could only do so much to protect what was left of her fragile spirit.

As the flames danced in the hearth of Barton's study, the quiet comfort of the night seemed at odds with the whirlwind that was about to be unleashed. Outside, the Pollock estate lay bathed in moonlight, a serene portrait of old money and inherited privilege. Inside, however, a darker, more sinister plan was beginning to take shape.

Barton Pollock, as ever, was untouched by sentimentality. His wife, his in-laws, even his newborn son, they were chess pieces on the board of life, and Barton knew better than to get lost in the mundane games of family affection. He was above that. He had always been above it.

He remained in his study, the heavy oak door closed, sealing him off from the world beyond. The flickering light of the fire cast a dark shadow as he reclined in his leather chair, the weight of his latest scheme swirling in his mind like the smooth whiskey in his glass. He lifted the receiver of his phone and dialed with calm precision, a number he'd committed to memory long ago.

At the other end, after just two rings, James Wilton's voice crackled through the receiver. "Good evening," came the clipped greeting.

"It's Barton." There was an implicit understanding between the two, this was no casual conversation. This was business, the kind of business that shaped futures and dictated the fate of nations, if only the pawns of the world knew it.

"James," Barton continued, leaning back further into the chair. The fire cast long, jagged shadows across his face as he spoke, his voice a velvet purr. "The wheels are turning, my friend. It seems our little proletariat is not as clueless as we'd hoped, and his working-class friends are likely no different."

There was a laugh from James at the other end, but it was bitter. "They're starting to think the system works for them. Can you believe it? They think their unions and middle-class salaries are secure, like they've somehow managed to tip the scales in their favor."

Barton's lip curled in distaste. "It's a dangerous illusion, that's what it is. They've gotten far too comfortable with this idea of fairness. Men like Jarod Davis, they actually believe they're in control of their destinies now. It's laughable, really. But it's also... problematic."

James paused, letting the thought hang between them. "So, what's your angle?"

Barton swirled his whiskey again, the ice clinking softly in the crystal tumbler. "Their strength is their unity. It's what makes them feel invincible. Weaken that unity, and they'll crumble. The trick, James, is to give them something to turn on each other over. A reason to doubt, to fear, and fear, as we both know, is the greatest motivator."

"And how do you propose we do that?" James asked, the intrigue in his voice evident.

Barton's smile widened, and for the first time this evening, his smile represented true joy. "We support the niggers."

There was a brief, disbelieving silence at the other end. Then, James spoke, his voice edged with curiosity. "You want us to support... civil rights?"

"Not openly," Barton clarified, his voice lowering to a conspiratorial whisper. "We don't want to be heroes of the movement. What we need is to secretly back the blacks cause. We give enough support to keep the momentum going, just enough to make progress attainable, but in reality, we're setting the stage for division."

James let out a thoughtful hum. "Division among the working class?"

"Exactly," Barton replied, his voice gaining confidence as he leaned forward, his eyes gleaming in the firelight. "We push for equal rights just enough to make the white working class uneasy. We make them believe that the government is no longer serving their interests, that they're being left behind while minorities are being elevated. What happens when a group that was once unified feels like their share of the pie is shrinking? They'll start turning on each other. The white workers will resent the jigaboos. They'll feel threatened, and that's when the cracks will start to show."

James chuckled softly. "Pitting them against one another."

Barton's smile was wolfish now. "Bigotry, James. It's always been the easiest weapon to wield. It doesn't require intelligence, just fear. The Nazis rose to power by giving the Germans a Jewish scapegoat. They didn't need to fix the economy; they just needed to redirect the anger, and it worked. Or look at the South, where segregation kept the poor whites and coons from uniting. The elites kept power by playing on racial fears, making sure the poor never realized they had the same enemy."

"And the best part?" Barton continued, his voice now a venomous whisper. "It's all irrational. They'll vote against their own interests, against the unions, against higher wages, because they'll be convinced they're fighting to protect what's *theirs*. We just need to make sure they believe that equality for one group means a loss for another."

James let out a long, slow breath. "It's a dangerous game. Nurturing fascism could have some serious ramifications for the country. But it's also brilliant. Use their fear, stoke the fires of bigotry, and sit back while they tear each other apart."

"That's the plan," Barton said, his voice as smooth as the whiskey he was savoring. "Let them destroy their own chances at prosperity, all while we remain untouched. When they've finished, when the dust settles, we'll still be here, wealthy, powerful, and beyond their reach. Our names will remain untarnished, while they're left picking up the pieces of their shattered dreams."

James was silent for a moment, then he let out a deep, satisfied breath. "I'll get things moving on my end. Let's see how quickly we can make them turn on each other."

Barton's smile faded slightly as he stared into the fire. "It'll happen faster than they think. Bigotry is a powerful tool, James. Always has been. We just need to make sure they're wielding it against each other."

The line clicked as James hung up, and Barton placed the receiver back on its cradle, the quiet of the study settling over him once more. He leaned back in his chair, watching the flames twist and flicker, feeling the warmth on his face as he considered the future. He had always known that real power wasn't in brute strength or even money, it was in controlling the narrative. Now, with his plan in motion, the working class would soon find themselves lost in the very divisions he had created.

He lifted his glass to his lips, savoring the last sip of whiskey, and set it down with a soft clink on the desk. Outside, the night was still and serene, the world oblivious to the storm that was about to be unleashed. Yet, somewhere in that same house, Jarod and Natalie held their grandson close, their hearts full of love and hope, unaware that the barrier known as Barton will force a wedge between them, his family, and their well-being. Barton was uninterested in indulging in family-love fantasies. He knew the truth of the world, that it was built on manipulation, on keeping people in their place, and a firm hand. With a final glance at the fire, Barton rose from his chair. There were more calls to make, more strings to pull. Wealth was, after all, a game that he intended to win.

Chapter 4: Waiting Outside

In the decade since Anthony's birth, the Pollock family settled into a routine that looked impeccable from the outside but hollowed out each of its members. Barton Pollock, ever the fixture of high society, maintained a pristine appearance, his suits pressed and his gaze unwavering. He was the man of his world, the man who knew every handshake, every face worth knowing. Yet his real passion lay far from the gala halls or family dinners. He craved influence, the intoxicating, invisible power of manipulating others to his will.

The Pollock home became a stage for Barton's ambition, a residence that echoed with polished marble and empty rooms. Barton had co-founded what he called a "think tank" with his old friend James Wilton, a group whose lofty title masked their true intent: using societal ideals to mask their pursuit of control. Barton relished those hours with James, drafting policies that served their own interests, crafting narratives to justify them, and refining their strategies for wielding power. And as he immersed himself in the ruthless world he had carefully crafted, his family became another pawn, a silent casualty of his ambitions.

For Sue, the home was her sanctuary and her prison. She floated from society luncheons to high-class gatherings, all the while shrouding herself in a daze of barbiturates and gin, escaping the hollow life she had drifted into. Motherhood had come and gone with the morning fog; a title she wore in name but rarely in practice. Instead, the nannies played her part, bringing Anthony up mechanically, filling his hours but never his heart. And Sue, absent, elegant, a perfect shadow of a wife, barely noticed she had a son at all.

Anthony roamed the Pollock estate with a familiar restlessness, a boy haunted by loneliness. The nannies dressed him, fed him, made sure he appeared for the occasional family photo or holiday card. But they didn't raise him. They were there to keep him out of sight and mind, as much a fixture of the household as the grandfather clock in the foyer. And as the nannies carried on their silent duties, Anthony found companionship in the television, that bright, comforting presence that hummed away the hours.

In the flickering light of the screen, Anthony's childhood unfolded. No one read him bedtime stories or tucked him in at night. Instead, cartoons lulled him to sleep. He drifted through his days, detached, invisible, except for rare moments when his parents' attention fell briefly upon him, only to flicker away again like an unfinished thought. School became a chore that reminded him of his failings, of how other children's worlds seemed to come alive with books and stories, while his own felt shrouded in static.

Yet, even as he floated between empty rooms, something in Anthony yearned for his father's approval. There were rare evenings, maybe once or twice a year, when Barton would smile at him, his expression tinged with pride, or what Anthony chose to see as pride. The family would occasionally gather to host important guests, high-society figures and dignitaries, and in these brief windows of connection, the Pollock home came alive. Sue's laughter filled the halls, Barton's voice softened, and Anthony felt a warmth he knew only in those fleeting moments. He began to live for those nights, craving the faint glow of family.

But tonight was different. Tonight, he would try to reach his father outside of any pretense. He had been waiting outside Barton's study for what felt like hours, listening to the murmur of his father's voice through the heavy wooden door. He pressed his ear against it, straining to catch snippets of Barton's low, commanding tone.

"...this new science, they call it global warming," Barton was saying, his voice cool, dismissive. "The public will eat it up, James, especially if we spin it right. The science itself isn't our concern, it's the panic it'll create. Imagine the oil companies, the energy sector, clawing for allies to fight this 'threat.' They'll need politicians in their pockets, and that's where we come in..."

After a brief pause, while Barton listened to the man he was conversing with on the phone, he continued, "...that doesn't concern me. Why should I worry about the future of other people's children? I'll be dead and gone before any real consequences take effect."

Anthony's heart raced. His father's words were powerful, controlled, as if he were guiding a secret web that held the world together. He didn't understand all of it, but he knew he wanted to be a part of that web, to become a part of his father's world.

The receiver clicked, and Anthony heard the slight rustle as his father ended the call. This was his moment. He took a deep breath and knocked softly on the door.

"Enter," came Barton's steady voice.

Anthony stepped inside, feeling small in the expanse of dark leather and polished wood. The study was as imposing as ever. The scent of old books and the faint smoke of his father's cigars filled the room. Barton looked up from his papers, his gaze piercing, assessing.

"Anthony," he said, a faint smile tugging at his lips, "what brings you here?"

Anthony felt his courage waver under that gaze, but he steadied himself. "I—I wanted to talk to you. About...about how to be successful."

Barton's eyebrows raised. For a moment, Anthony felt he'd struck the wrong chord. But then Barton's smile returned, sharper this time, as if he had been waiting for this. He leaned back in his chair, folding his hands in front of him.

"Successful, is it?" His voice was almost amused. "That's a tall order, Anthony. But I suppose it's never too early to start learning."

Anthony's heart pounded with anticipation. He had imagined this moment so many times, dreamed of his father sharing some secret wisdom, of becoming his apprentice in this grand, unseen world.

Barton's expression grew contemplative, and when he spoke again, his tone was measured, instructive. "Success isn't about what you know," Barton said, his voice firm, steady. "It's about who you know and how they see you. People don't care if you're smart. They care if you're impressive. If you walk into a room and make them believe you know everything, then you do."

Anthony paused, trying to absorb this. "So... I don't need to be smart?"

Barton snickered, with a low, almost indulgent sound. "What is 'smart,' really? Memorize as much as you can, and you'll convince everyone that you're the smartest person in the room. Here." He pulled a thick, leather-bound book from his shelf and pushed it across the desk toward Anthony.

This precious book, filled with facts and strange bits of knowledge, was heavy in Anthony's hands.

Barton's eyes held a rare glint of something close to pride. "Learn these," he said. "Memorize what's interesting, that's what sets you apart. Then, when you speak, they'll see you as indispensable."

Anthony held the book close, feeling the weight of his father's approval like a gift.

Barton continued, his voice lowering, carrying a hint of warmth that was almost foreign. "Remember, Anthony, life is about impressions. Make the right ones, and you'll never have to worry about the rest."

"Oh, one more thing, if you can get away without paying for goods or services, don't. Only idiots insist on being honest. Cutthroat selfishness is the real path to wealth and power. We call it just 'doing business.'"

Anthony's heart swelled. In this moment, he felt as if he had unlocked some forbidden door. He had entered his father's carefully constructed world. And in that world, he sensed his place, his purpose: to be seen, to be known, to become the person his father wanted him to be, to become powerful.

Barton leaned back, studying him. "Anything else?"

Anthony hesitated, feeling the urge to say something, anything that might keep his father's attention. But the moment had passed. He knew it, and so did Barton. Anthony simply shook his head and turned to leave while clutching the book as if it held every answer he'd ever sought.

A sense of purpose welled within him as he stepped out of the study. He understood what his father had tried to teach him. Life was about appearances, about convincing others of a carefully shaped truth. In that quiet moment Anthony vowed to live by his father's rules. He'd become a captivating man whose mere presence impresses the masses.

As Anthony exited, he felt the hollow ache of something missing. It was something unspoken that unmistakably lingered in the spaces between their words. His opportunity to bond with his father closed with the door he just walked out of.

It was a bright spring day in New York City, the hustle-and-bustle carried the promise of excitement. The Pollock family traveled to the city for what, on the surface, appeared to be a glamorous excursion. They would stay a few days in the heart of the "Big Apple", at the Ritz-Carlton, and for Sue, a discreet visit to an exclusive clinic specializing in cosmetic surgery. The whole trip was Barton's idea that he casually proposed over dinner a few weeks ago. Sue agreed without hesitation. In her world, appearances were everything, and the thought of refining her already elegant features felt like the natural next step for a socialite of her standing. For Barton, it was another move in maintaining his facade of perfection. Sue's looks were an extension of his image, and in his mind, his trophy needed to remain polished.

While Sue recovered in a private suite, swathed in luxury and hidden from prying eyes, Barton found himself in an unusual position; he was responsible for Anthony's care. It wasn't a role he relished, but necessity had placed him there and Barton wasn't one to sidestep responsibility.

On the other hand, Anthony was thrilled. At twelve years old, time alone with his father was a rare occurrence, and the idea of spending the day with his father filled him with excitement. In Anthony's eyes, Barton was the pinnacle of success. He was a man who navigated life with confidence that seemed almost mythical. Barton's attention was a prize that Anthony craved, though it usually was out of reach.

As their chauffeur drove through the crowded streets, Barton remained silent, his eyes scanned the passing pedestrians with disdain; he was above such labors. Anthony sat beside him, his heart pounding, wondering what his father had planned. Barton had mentioned only that it would be "a gift," a phrase that carried weight coming from a man like him.

When the limousine finally pulled up to the curb, Anthony's eyes widened as he read the words on the towering building in front of them. Carnegie Hall. The famous place etched in his memory from his big book of trivial facts Barton had gifted him. He could hardly believe it, Carnegie Hall. The name itself held a kind of magic. It was where legendary performers came to showcase their gifts.

"This way," Barton said, his voice calm, though there was an unmistakable authority in it as he stepped on to the sidewalk. Anthony followed in a daze, the realization of where they were was slowly sinking in. Carnegie Hall wasn't open to the public outside of performances, and yet here they were, as though they owned the place.

Barton exchanged a few quiet words with a man at the entrance, and just like that, the heavy doors swung open, ushering them inside the hallowed space. Anthony's sneakers squeaked on the polished hardwood floor as they entered the grand foyer. The hall's immaculate decor was impressive. The aurora was thick with the memory of all the great performances that had taken place there. Anthony felt a sense of awe wash over him.

Barton moved with his usual unhurried confidence, hands in his pockets as if this were just another errand. He didn't offer any explanation, and Anthony knew better than to ask for one; he had learned by now that his father revealed things in his own time.

They made their way into the main hall, and Anthony gasped. The space was vast, larger than he had imagined, with rows of seats stretching into dimness. The stage gleamed under the downlights, a polished expanse of maple that seemed to command attention.

Barton stopped near the center of the hall and turned to Anthony, his eyes glinting with a faint smile. "Sing," he said.

Anthony was caught off guard. "What?"

"Sing something," Barton repeated, his voice even and patient. "You're standing in Carnegie Hall, so sing."

Anthony paused while his heart pounded. He had never sung in front of his father. The idea of doing so here, in this legendary place, was intimidating, but Barton's expression carried that air of expectation, and Anthony didn't want to disappoint him.

Taking a deep breath, Anthony started to sing the first song that came to mind. It was a simple tune that he had often heard on the radio. His voice wavered at first, shaky with nerves, but as it filled the hall, something extraordinary happened. The acoustics of Carnegie Hall were unlike anything he had experienced. His voice, small and uncertain, echoed off the walls and returned to him richer and fuller, almost as if the hall itself was amplifying his effort.

As he sang, his nervousness began to ease. The space and his song made him feel like part of something larger than himself, like he was somehow connected to the countless performances that had echoed through the legendary hall. When he finished, his last note sung, there was a profound silence. It was a silence that felt as though the walls themselves were waiting for applause.

Barton nodded with a small glint of satisfaction in his eyes. He stepped forward and placed a hand on Anthony's shoulder, his touch was firm but brief. "Well done," he said.

Anthony's chest swelled with pride. His father, who so rarely offered praise, had acknowledged his effort, but it was Barton's next words that would stay with Anthony for the rest of his life.

"You've just sung at Carnegie Hall," Barton said, his voice low and matter-of-fact.

Anthony stared at his father, letting the weight of those words sink in. It hadn't dawned on him at first, but now it was clear; this wasn't just a gift, it was a lesson. Barton wasn't concerned with the truth of the moment, whether or not Anthony's song had deserved a Carnegie invitation, or that no one had been there to hear it. What mattered was Anthony could now claim his talents reached all the way to Carnegie Hall, and that, in Barton's world, had real value.

"You can now tell your people," Barton continued, his voice smooth and instructive, "that you've performed here. It doesn't matter that the hall was empty, or that only your father was listening. What matters is that you were here singing. That's the story. That's what they'll remember. Let them embellish the story themselves."

Anthony was struck. His father had always known how to shape reality, to control the narrative, to make people see what he wanted them to see, and now, he was teaching Anthony to do the same.

This was more than just a moment, it was a defining moment.

Anthony followed his father out of the hall, his mind buzzing with the revelation that he had sung at Carnegie Hall. In Barton's world, and now Anthony's, that was all that mattered.

Back at the hotel, Anthony couldn't stop replaying the day in his mind. The hall, the song, the lesson. It was intoxicating, the idea that with the right words, the right framing, you could be anyone, anywhere.

Anthony had sung at Carnegie Hall, and from now on, no one needs to know any more details than that.

Middle school was a complicated place for Anthony. He recently started going by "Tony" in an effort to shed the formal stiffness that had always followed him. It was a move designed to help him fit in, to sound more like one of the guys, but fitting in was harder than just changing a name. Tony wasn't exactly popular. He wasn't the most attractive or charming, nor did he have the athletic prowess of some of the other boys. His interests skewed toward trivial obscure facts and a habit of boasting about himself that made him come off as more of a joke than he realized. Still, he managed to be widely accepted as "OK," hovering somewhere in the middle of the social hierarchy.

Puberty arrived like a freight train and with it came new and confusing desires. Tony was obsessing over girls in a way that was both thrilling and frustrating. They intrigued and fascinated him, yet they seemed forever out of reach. He watched as his classmates began to pair off and awkwardly stumble through the early stages of flirting and dating. It was different for Tony. He was deeply interested in the girls, but the interest wasn't reciprocated, at least not with the girls he wished to date. The girls didn't dislike him, they just didn't seem to see him at all.

One day, after lunch Tony used the bathroom for a moment of solitude. It was common for him to retreat there, away from the noise and chaos of the cafeteria, where he could collect his thoughts and escape the awkwardness of social interactions. He entered the stall, locked the door, then sat down. That's when he noticed it. There was a crude drawing of a naked woman etched into the partition. The image was nothing more than a rough collection of curves scratched into the paint by some boy with a dirty mind and too much time on his hands. But for Tony, it was the most exciting thing he'd ever seen. He stared at it, his heart pounding, his adolescent mind whirling with thoughts he didn't fully understand. He had never seen a naked woman before, not even in magazines. This rough amateur sketch was enough to ignite something inside him.

Before he knew it Tony's pants were down, and his hands moved of their own accord. His body responded to the overwhelming surge of hormones and curiosity. He was lost in the moment, completely absorbed, jerking off to this primitive image.

What he didn't notice was that someone else had entered the bathroom.

Mark Fields was the last person Tony wanted to encounter in this vulnerable moment. Unfortunately for Tony, he just so happened to walk in unannounced. Mark was notorious for sticking his nose in places it didn't belong. He was loud, obnoxious, and took special pleasure in embarrassing other kids. And now, he was standing just outside Tony's stall hearing his pleasure taking place. Mark leaped at this opportunity. His keen eyes darted to the gap between the stall door.

"Whoa, what's going on in there?" Mark's gleeful voice boomed through the bathroom. This was his greatest discovery. "That must be the smallest dick in the world." Tony froze, horror washing over him as he fumbled to pull his pants back up with trembling hands.

Mark wasn't done. He leaned in closer while peering through the crack with a wicked grin spreading across his face. "Oh man, bopping the world's smallest slice of bologna." Mark's howling laughter echoed off the tiled walls, amplifying the cruelty. "Tiny Tony!" Mark declared as though he had just struck gold. "That's what I'm gonna call you from now on—Tiny Tony! Wait 'til everyone hears about this!"

Tony's heart sank. He wanted to scream and beg Mark to shut up or to deny everything, but he couldn't. His mouth was dry and his hands clumsy as he tried to fix his clothes while his mind raced. Mark's laughter felt like knives slicing through his skin and Tony knew, without a doubt, that this was a moment he'd never be able to escape.

By the end of the day the whole school knew. The rumors spread like wildfire. Mark's loudmouth, and everyone's eagerness for a new piece of gossip, devastated Tony. He could hear the whispers and snickers everywhere he went. That awful Tiny Tony nickname followed him from class to class, from hallway to hallway. He tried to deny it, but Mark's story had taken root. His classmates, always eager for a new target, latched onto it with glee.

That evening, Tony returned home in a state of quiet devastation. He couldn't hide it. The humiliation clung to him like a second skin. He wanted to disappear, to start over, to go anywhere but back to that school. But more than anything, he needed help, he needed his father.

After dinner, Tony approached Barton's study, he could hear the murmur of his father's conversation through the cracked door as he lingered outside, too afraid to interrupt and too desperate to walk away.

"Yes, the Vietnam War has been a setback," Barton was saying, his tone clipped but measured. "Public sentiment turned, and that weakened our position, no doubt. But there's an opportunity here. The defense contractors have taken a hit; they need allies now more than ever and you know what that means...campaign contributions."

There was a pause as Barton listened to the other voice on the line, his fingers tapping rhythmically on the desk.

"Exactly. If we can secure their backing, we can turn this around. Their money can fuel the campaigns of our politicians, the ones who know how to reframe the narrative. War or no war, we just need to keep the machine running. Defense is always a business, and business should always be booming."

He chuckled softly, the sound unsettling in its calculated detachment. "They need us just as much as we need them. All we must do is remind them of that."

After Barton hung up the phone he could hear Tony, in a meek tone, call to him outside the door, "father."

"What is it?" Barton asked, his voice sharp, already weary of whatever trivial complaint Tony might have. "Come in here to speak with me."

"I have a problem," Tony said, his voice small, as though it were too painful to let the words out.

Barton sighed, setting down his pen and leaning back in his chair. "Go on, then."

Tony hesitated, then spilled everything. He told his father about the incident in the bathroom, about Mark's mocking, about the nickname, and about how it had spread through the school. He was ruined. His voice wavered as he spoke with shame palpable in every word. "I...Dad, I can't go back there," Tony stammered, his voice barely above a whisper. "Please, can I change schools? I can't...I can't face them."

For a moment, Barton was silent, staring at Tony with an expression that was hard to read. Then, slowly, a cold, hard grimace spread across his face. "No," Barton said, his voice calm but firm.

Tony stood there stunned. "But—"

"You're not changing schools," Barton interrupted. "Your school is the finest in the area. You're not running away from this."

"But Dad, I can't..."

"I don't care about your happiness, Anthony." Barton's voice cut through the air like a knife. "This isn't about you. It's about *me*. You're at that school for a reason. It's the best in the area and *I* need to be able to boast about it. If you switch schools people will talk. They'll wonder why and that reflects on me. I can't have people thinking my son is common or flawed."

Tony felt the weight of his father's words settle on him like a stone. Barton's cold and detached tone left no room for argument. This wasn't about his well-being. This wasn't about what he needed. It was about Barton's reputation, about maintaining the image of a perfect, successful family.

"If you can't handle it," Barton continued, his eyes narrowing, "there's always military school. Plenty of other rich kids who serve no purpose to their parents end up there. Is that what you want?"

Tony shook his head, his face flushed with shame and fear.

"No? Good." Barton leaned forward, his voice lowering. "Now, I have a solution. Listen closely." Tony swallowed, his heart still racing.

"You'll be provided with pornographic magazines. I'll make sure you get them. They stay in your room, and you only look at them with the door shut by yourself. Understood? That should quench your lusty appetite. And you never let anyone see your peter ever again." Tony nodded, being awarded some smut sounded pretty good.

"You go back to being called Anthony. The nickname 'Tiny Tony' doesn't have as much punch if you're not Tony anymore." Again, Anthony nodded, though the thought of abandoning the name he had worked so hard to make his own felt like a defeat.

"You deny it ever happened. Deny, deny, deny. And while you're at it, accuse the boy...Mark, was it?...of being an untrustworthy goon. Make sure everyone knows he can't be trusted. People will start questioning his version of events. That's how you handle this."

Tony stood there. The magnitude of Barton's plan settled over him like a blanket of cold inevitability. His father's words were harsh but effective. Barton didn't care about fixing the problem, all he cared about was controlling the narrative, and protecting the family's reputation. As much as he hated it, Tony knew he had no choice but to follow his father's plan.

The next day, Tony became Anthony again, doing his best to deny the rumors and smear Mark's reputation as an unreliable loudmouth. The plan worked to a degree. The rumor lost some of its momentum, but it never truly died. In the back of his peers' minds, he will always be Tiny Tony, the boy with a tiny pecker who flies solo in the bathroom stall.

As the days turned into weeks, and the weeks into months, Anthony began to realize something that had always been lurking in the back of his mind. His relationship with his father was one-sided. Barton didn't care about Anthony's happiness, his struggles, or his fears. All that mattered to him was that Anthony represented an image he could boast about. If Barton couldn't find things to brag about, Anthony's future would be as cold and lonely as a soldier assigned to an Arctic outpost.

Anthony Pollock sat in his high school auditorium, surrounded by the excited hum of his classmates. His graduation ceremony was underway. Names were called and diplomas handed out while cameras flashed in the audience. Yet, despite the celebratory atmosphere, Anthony's mind wandered. As he waited for his name to be called, he couldn't help but reflect on the last few years. His reputation still followed him like a shadow he couldn't shake.

Tiny Tony.

It was a nickname born from a humiliating moment in middle school that followed him through the halls of his high school. He tried to shed it by going back to "Anthony," by denying it ever happened, by doing everything his father had advised. However, the whispers never truly faded. His peers didn't mock him outright anymore, but the ghost of Tiny Tony lingered in the background of every interaction and every attempt to fit in. It wasn't just the nickname that held him back, it was the stigma that came with it, and the way it had eroded his self-confidence, especially when it came to girls.

Anthony never dated. He helplessly watched from the sidelines as his classmates fumbled through their high school romances, awkward and brief as they were. He had never been part of that world. His father's advice, his short stature, the magazines hidden away in his room, and the shame he still carried had kept him isolated. He had withdrawn only to focus on maintaining his reputation and staying out of situations that might expose his vulnerability. High school had been something to endure and not enjoy.

But now, as the principal called out his name..."Anthony Pollock"...he walked across the stage to receive his diploma. He heard someone call out "Go Tiny," and felt a strange mix of emotions. It was over. High school, the place that had solidified him as Tiny Tony, was behind him. He was no longer a boy caught in the humiliations of adolescence. He was a graduate. A man, or at least the beginnings of one. In a few short months, he would be leaving it all behind as he moved on to something greater. Today, Tiny Tony was no more.

After the ceremony, Barton was waiting for him, dressed impeccably in a tailored suit that seemed out of place among the crowd of families in their casual summer attire. His handshake was firm, his smile thin but approving.

"Congratulations, Anthony," Barton said, his voice even and controlled, as always. "You've done well... enough."

It was typical of Barton to deliver praise with a caveat. Anthony nodded while feeling the familiar twinge of both pride and disappointment that came with his father's approval. Barton pulled him aside, away from the milling crowd, his expression grew more serious.

"There's something you need to know," Barton began, with measured tone. "I pulled some strings for you. You've been accepted to Harvard."

Anthony's heart leaped. Harvard! The name alone carried so much prestige, of success, of doors opening in places that would remain locked to most people. He knew his grades weren't enough to get him in on his own merit. His father had orchestrated this for him. Barton used his connections and his influence to make sure Anthony was placed in the world's most distinguished university.

"It's a gift," Barton continued, his eyes sharp. "Probably the last one you'll get from me."

Anthony's excitement faltered. "The last one?"

Barton nodded with an unflinching expression. "The family fortune isn't what it once was. Socialist government handouts have made sure of that. There won't be much left by the time I'm gone. You won't be inheriting anything significant, if anything at all. So don't expect to."

He paused, glancing out the window before adding, "That said, we've managed to get our man into the White House. If he's successful in pushing through our agenda of lower taxes and less government interference, there might be something left, but there's headwinds. The public's appetite for welfare and regulations is going to make it a challenge. Still, if he can shift the tide, we might be able to salvage a bit of our fortune."

Anthony felt the weight of his father's words. Barton wasn't planning to leave behind a legacy for his son, he was spending it all now, living the life he wanted, with no thought for the future. But there was a silver lining.

"Harvard will be paid for," Barton added, as though that alone should be enough. "You won't have to worry about that."

It was a crushing revelation but an undeniable gift nonetheless. Getting into Harvard was a dream that most people couldn't even imagine, and it was Anthony's reality now. Paid for, secured, with no questions asked. But the purpose of that gift was clear: Barton had given him this opportunity, not for Anthony's sake, but for his own. He could boast about it. He could say his son was a Harvard man, and that was all that mattered.

The summer passed in a blur of preparations. Anthony found himself alternating between excitement and dread. The thought of escaping his high school reputation and starting fresh at Harvard filled him with hope, but there was also the pressure of living up to his father's expectations. Barton's presence would loom over everything, even from a distance.

As August drew to a close, Anthony packed his bags and moved to Cambridge. The ancient buildings, cobblestone streets, and the aura of intellect and achievement were intoxicating. But soon after he arrived reality set in. Harvard was as daunting as it was reputable, and Anthony came to realize that his high school academics left him in a precarious position.

During registration, it was clear that his options were limited. He had hoped to pursue law or medicine. Those fields would impress Barton and give him something tangible to boast about, while simultaneously filling his own pockets. Unfortunately, his high school transcript was lacking. He simply didn't have the grades or the background to qualify for Harvard's medical or law programs.

Sitting in the registrar's office and feeling the weight of the decision pressing down on him, Anthony didn't know what to do. His mind raced with the same thoughts over and over. It must be something impressive that my father can brag about.

After an exhausting round of conversations with various administrators, he was eventually sent to speak with a counselor. The kind-eyed older woman sat across from him while assessing his transcript carefully. She looked up with a soft but direct expression. "Anthony, I think we need to be realistic about your options. Medical school or law school are not within reach given your academic history."

Anthony shifted uncomfortably in his seat. "I know," he muttered. "But my major needs to be... something important and impressive."

The counselor sighed gently. She was clearly exhausted by students trying to navigate the pressures of parental expectations. "There are plenty of other options. We could explore some of the humanities, maybe something in sociology, or literature. What about history?" Anthony shook his head. "It needs to be something my father can boast about," he insisted. "It needs to sound... significant."

She leaned back while tapping her pen against her desk thoughtfully. "Well, there's a program in Physical Therapy. It's technically a medical discipline, though not the same as becoming a doctor or a surgeon. However, there is demand for it, and it has the medical component you're looking for."

Anthony frowned, unsure. Physical Therapy? It wasn't law or medicine. It sounded like a nurse, a job reserved for women. However, it came with a medical title. That could work, couldn't it? Barton would be able to say his son was pursuing a career in healthcare, and that was something to boast about.

"You'd qualify for it," the counselor added. "The program is growing, and there's a lot of potential there."

Anthony nodded slowly while realizing that this might be his best option. It wasn't exactly what he had imagined for himself, but it ticked enough boxes. It had prestige in its own way. "I'll do it," he said, his voice quiet but resolute.

"Physical Therapy, then," the counselor said, cementing it in stone before he could change his mind. "It's a good choice, Anthony. You're making a smart decision."

As Anthony left the office, he walked through the storied halls of Harvard. He couldn't shake the strange mix of emotions roiling inside him. He was here. He was at Harvard, the place people dreamed of. But once again, his life had been shaped not by his own desires and accomplishments, but by the expectations of his father. The realization settled over him, with a familiar heaviness, that his life wasn't entirely his own.

Chapter 8: The Perfect Plan

By the time Anthony reached his upperclassman years at Harvard, he had come to terms with the rhythm of his life. His academic success was middling, nothing that would impress his father, but still, it wasn't an outright failure. He was on track to graduate from the Physical Therapy program on time, which was a legitimate enough field for a man with his background. It wasn't law or medicine, the types of fields that commanded universal respect, but it was still respectable enough that Barton could brag about it at social events.

Romance was one glaring void in Anthony's life. He saw it all around him everywhere. His classmates strolled through Harvard Yard, hand-in-hand, then got intimate in dorm rooms late at night. He was always an observer, always just on the outside, never part of that world. The coeds didn't flirt with the short guys, and after the humiliations of his teen-aged years, he didn't dare approach them. The last thing he wanted was for the ghost of "Tiny Tony" to resurface. He would have none of that again, not in Harvard's prestigious social circles. But there was something else gnawing at him, a worry that lingered far more than his previous nickname. People might start whispering that he was gay, a "closet queer," as some had crudely put it before.

The whispers and assumptions needed to be shut down. He wasn't interested in men, but the speculation could ruin him, especially in his father's eyes. Barton had always made it clear that the Pollock name was about power, money, and legacy, which aren't exactly qualities associated with a man who can't get a girlfriend.

Anthony knew he had to find a wife. Not just a girlfriend, but a wife. A partner who could offer him stability and respectability his father had always demanded. Someone who wouldn't leave when she discovered the truth about his awkwardness, his insecurities, and his underwhelming weenis.

Harvard wasn't the place to find her. The women there were too ambitious, too driven, the kind of people who might see through his facade. Anthony couldn't afford to be with someone who would challenge him or ask too many questions. He needed someone who would fall for his boasts and wouldn't poke at his cracks. It dawned on him, church was the answer.

Anthony wasn't religious. Barton had always scoffed at religion being the working-man's form of science. But church was where young Christian women could be found. A woman who would believe in the sanctity of marriage and would find an educated man like Anthony, on the path to a respectable career and seemingly devout, irresistible. It didn't matter that he had no real faith. This was part of his strategy and Anthony was becoming strategic.

So, he began attending a small church away from Harvard's campus. It was filled with young ladies, most of whom were still clinging to their ideals of chastity and purity. Anthony played the part well. He spoke of his future as a "medical professional," conveniently inflating his role in physical therapy. He threw in trivia facts that he had memorized from Barton's book, knowing that people often mistook the ability to recite random information for intelligence, and, of course, he never hesitated to mention that he had once sung at Carnegie Hall. Even though the story was heavily embellished, it never failed to impress.

That's when he met Caroline.

Caroline was exactly what Anthony had been searching for. She was pretty, quiet, and devout. She was the perfect blend of simplicity and loyalty. She had grown up in a small town, and her ambitions were modest. Caroline wasn't looking for a career, independence, or even excitement. All she wanted was to become a wife, and in Anthony, she saw a man who could give her that.

Anthony courted her with precision, using every tool Barton had taught him: boast, impress, control the narrative. He exaggerated his academic achievements, downplayed his insecurities, and crafted an image of a man who was going places. Caroline never questioned it. In her eyes, Anthony was a man destined for greatness and marrying him meant security, stability, and status. To her, he was the ultimate prize. He was a man on the verge of a medical career who could provide her with the life she had always dreamed of.

Within three months, they were married.

The wedding was small and modest, exactly as Anthony had planned. Caroline's family adored him, thinking she had hit the jackpot with a Harvard man who had a bright future ahead of him. Anthony's parents, Barton and Sue, attended but stayed only long enough to fulfill their family obligation. Barton, as expected, had little interest in mingling with Caroline's working-class family. The very sight of them made Barton uneasy, and after a brief appearance at the ceremony, he made an excuse to leave early, dragging Sue with him.

Anthony watched as his father walked out of the chapel. He had hoped this marriage would change things. He hoped that Barton would finally be proud of him and want to know him. After all, he was settled down with a wife and a blossoming career on the way. He wasn't gay. He wasn't the "Tiny Tony" his father might have worried about. He was a married man, building a life. It didn't matter. The indifference in Barton's eyes was clear. Barton had never cared about Anthony's happiness, he only cared about appearances, and Anthony's marriage was just another formality.

Still, as he looked at Caroline, beaming in her wedding dress, Anthony felt a twinge of pride. He had done it. He had secured a pretty wife, and now, the whispers would finally stop. No one could accuse him of being anything less than a real man.

Unfortunately, Anthony quickly discovered that marriage was not as easy as he thought it would be.

On their honeymoon, the reality of his life became painfully clear. His intimacy issues were impossible to ignore. Anthony had spent years addicted to porn which was the only form of intimacy he had ever really known. His understanding of sex had been shaped by a lifetime of fantasies that bore no resemblance to reality. He had no idea how to connect with Caroline in any meaningful way.

Their first night together was awkward and unfulfilling. Anthony treated it like a task. It was something to check off a list rather than an act of passion. Caroline, naive and inexperienced, chalked it up to wedding night nerves, but as the weeks went on, it became clear that Anthony's issues may run deeper.

Anthony had been deeply affected by years of pornography. The fantasy of it created a detachment from reality. His sexual encounters with Caroline were mechanical, brief, and devoid of any real passion. Caroline never experienced an orgasm with him. Although she didn't fully understand what she was missing, she knew something was wrong. Anthony's manhood simply wasn't capable of providing her with the pleasure she had hoped for, and his emotional distance left her feeling more alone than ever.

To make matters worse, Caroline noticed Anthony's wandering eye. Whenever they were out in public, he couldn't help but compare her to other women. He'd subtly glance at women in ways that made Caroline feel inadequate. She noticed how he looked at them and how his eyes lingered a little too long. It was as though he was constantly searching for something else, something better, something he would never see in her.

Anthony, for his part, was satisfied. He had accomplished his goal. He was married. His father and peers couldn't accuse him of being gay or unmanly now. He had fulfilled the role he had been born to play.

However, as the months went on, the cracks in his marriage began to show. Caroline, once so full of hope, now found herself feeling trapped.

She started to wonder if she made a hasty mistake. She married for security and status, much like Sue, her mother-in-law, had done before her. She didn't fully understand what her marriage lacked. The riches and comfort Anthony had promised came at a cost. There was no real love between them, no genuine connection. Anthony's attention wandered, and his inability to satisfy her emotionally or physically left her feeling empty. Divorce was out of the question; her faith wouldn't allow it. Like Sue, Caroline was trapped in a marriage that had been built on illusion.

Anthony, meanwhile, found himself falling into the same patterns as his father. He married to fulfill an image and to give his life the appearance of success and respectability, but he hadn't truly found happiness. He spent his days working towards his degree and his evenings with Caroline, going through the motions of a marriage that had never been built on love, trust, or compatibility.

In the end, Anthony had achieved exactly what he had set out to do. He found a wife who wouldn't leave him, wouldn't challenge him, and would stay by his side even as the emptiness of their relationship grew more apparent each passing day. But, like Barton before him, Anthony realized that attaining an image wasn't the same as finding fulfillment.

Chapter 9: Budding Maturity

The sun beamed over Harvard Yard, casting light and shadow across the old brick buildings. Graduation day. Anthony Pollock, finally draped in a cap and gown, stood among his classmates. On this special day, a grin stretched ear to ear. He'd reached the finish line. "Tiny Tony" was gone. Today, he was Anthony Pollock, Harvard graduate, and the title felt like armor.

His name echoed across the lawn, ushering Anthony to the stage. He shook hands with the university president and accepted his diploma, letting the applause wash over him like a warm wave. This moment belonged to him. He worked for it all on his own. No one could touch it. Glancing at the crowd, he couldn't help but search for his absent parents. Barton did send a telegram, a cold afterthought, and Sue was oblivious of his whereabouts. They hadn't come for him, not now or ever. But today, he refused to let that dim his pride.

After the ceremony, Caroline appeared from the crowd. She threw her arms around him, her face all lit up with pride. "You did it!" she said, squeezing him tight.

"We did it," he replied, managing a soft smile. Caroline had become his anchor, holding him steady through that last year. Their marriage had started out as a convenience, a way to gain some stability, but she had proven herself in ways he hadn't expected.

They walked through campus hand in hand, letting the excitement of the day surround them. Anthony felt something resembling joy, a rare swell of optimism. He'd secured a position at a respected clinic in Boston, a solid start to his career, with stability and a touch of prestige. He hadn't expected to relish helping people, but guiding patients through recovery stirred a quiet satisfaction he hadn't anticipated. For once, his path seemed promising.

Within weeks, he found his footing at the clinic. His days brimmed with purpose as he helped patients regain strength, watching as they celebrated small victories. His colleagues respected him, and the work itself felt steady. Here, he wasn't just Barton's son or some afterthought. He was himself. He was wanted.

But at home, Caroline had started hinting at a different future, one he hadn't planned for.

"I think it's time we had a baby," she said over dinner, her voice bright with hope.

Anthony froze, his fork halfway to his mouth. "A baby?" he asked, trying to keep his cool.

"Yes!" she said as her eyes lit up. "We're settled now. You've got a great job. We have a nice apartment... it's the perfect time."

He forced a laugh, attempting to mask his discomfort. "Maybe in a few months," he said, hoping she'd let it drop. "I'm still getting into the swing of things at work."

But Caroline didn't let it drop. She mentioned it here and there, hopeful looks slipping into conversations, her words gentle but insistent. The idea felt like a trap slowly closing around him.

Anthony couldn't imagine himself as a father. But Caroline's disappointment gnawed at him, and eventually, he agreed to try.

Months passed, and her eagerness turned to concern. One night, as they sat down to dinner, she looked at him carefully, her fork set aside. "Maybe we should see a doctor," she said, her voice soft but sure.

Anthony's stomach twisted. "We don't need to worry yet. These things take time."

But she didn't back down, and soon they found themselves in a specialist's office. The testing period felt like an eternity. A week later, they returned to hear the results.

Dr. Whitman, a man with steady eyes and a kind face, cleared his throat as he looked at them. "Anthony, Caroline," he began. "We need to talk about the results of your tests."

"What is it?" Anthony asked, keeping his voice steady despite the knot forming in his stomach.

Dr. Whitman shifted his gaze to Anthony. "You have a condition called congenital hypogonadism. Your reproductive organs didn't fully develop during puberty."

The words landed like a punch. Anthony felt heat rush to his face, his hands going cold. "What... what does that mean?" he asked, though the answer felt clear as day.

The doctor spoke with calm finality. "It means that, unfortunately, you're unlikely to father children naturally. It's not that you have no chance, it's just the chances are slim. Your sperm count is about half of what is typical, and their movement is only at 10%, when we like to see at least 40%. Your best bet is to let your sperm supply peak and hope the timing is right. It will require about 60 days or so to fully supply your testicles with enough sperm to impregnate. However, that amount of abstinence and timing is quite unrealistic."

Caroline sucked in a breath, her hand flew to her mouth, and tears filled her eyes. "But... isn't there anything we can do?" she asked as her voice broke.

Dr. Whitman nodded. "There are options—fertility treatments, assisted reproductive technologies—but I'll be honest, the chances remain low. I'd suggest taking time to process this. We can discuss options after you've had some time to think this over."

The ride home passed in silence. Caroline stared out the window, tears streaking her cheeks, while Anthony gripped the wheel, his mind spinning. He felt a sense of relief laced with shame. He never wanted children, yet the diagnosis stung, tugged at places he didn't want exposed.

Back home, Caroline finally broke the silence. "I want to consider adoption," she said, her voice soft but firm.

He looked up, with surprise in his eyes. "Adoption?"

"Yes." She didn't waver as she gazed straight into his soul. "I want to be a mother, Anthony. If we can't have a biological child, let's give a child a loving home."

His stomach turned. "I don't know if that's a good idea."

"Why not?" she pressed, her voice calm but resolute.

"It's just... it's complicated." The words felt clumsy, hollow. How would his father look at him now? Raising someone else's child, failing to produce his own heir.

Caroline's gaze didn't let up. "Families are built on love, Anthony. Genetics aren't everything."

He sighed, frustration spilling over. "Maybe we need more time to think about it. I'm just getting started in my career, and adoption... that's a lot to take on."

Her eyes didn't leave him, calm but edged with steel. "I know your career matters, but this matters to me. I want more than just us, Anthony. I need more."

He stood and started pacing the room, feeling the walls close in around him. "Why can't we be happy with what we have? Things are good. Why risk that?"

Her voice, barely a whisper, held firm. "It's not enough for me."

Frustration surged in him. "Why are you pushing this? We're fine the way we are."

Her tears glinted under the dome kitchen light, but her voice didn't waver. "Fine for you, maybe. I'm trying to share what I need, but you won't listen."

He looked away, unwilling to meet her eyes. "I just don't think it's the right time."

She took a steady breath. "I'm going to investigate it. I hope you'll join me, but I can't wait forever."

Her words struck him like a blow. He didn't want children, had never wanted them, but the thought of losing Caroline sent a jolt through him. She had become his anchor, the one constant in his life he could rely on.

For weeks, tension hung between them. Caroline threw herself into research, meeting with adoption agencies, while Anthony buried himself in work. The clinic became his escape, a place where he felt competent and respected, where everything made sense. But every night, he returned home to a silence that weighed on him, a reminder of what he was risking.

One evening, he walked in to find her at the kitchen table, papers spread out in front of her. She looked up, her eyes bright with a quiet hope. "I spoke with an agency today," she said. "They think we'd be a good fit."

He sighed, setting his briefcase down. "Caroline, we've been over this."

She didn't look away. "No, you've been avoiding it. Just look at the information. If you still feel the same, then we'll talk."

Reluctantly, he sat down, his stomach knotted with unease. "Fine. Show me."

She laid out the agency's approach, her voice firm but hopeful. They specialized in placing infants with couples who couldn't conceive, guiding them through every step, offering support that lasts long after the placement. As she spoke, he felt something inside him shift.

"This could be our chance," she said, her voice quiet. "A chance to have a family."

He rubbed his temples, the weight of it pressing down on him. "I just... I don't know, Caroline. What if I can't be the father this child needs?"

Her hand found his, steady and warm. "We'll do this together, Anthony. You don't have to do it alone."

He looked into her eyes, saw the love and determination there, and felt his resistance start to crack. She wanted this, deeply. And he knew that if he kept resisting, he might lose her. Maybe, just maybe, this was a chance to create something new, something that didn't carry his father's shadow.

"Alright," he said, his voice rough. "Let's take the first step. Together."

Relief overcame her and she smiled, her voice dropping with gratitude. "Thank you," she whispered.

The road tested them both. The interviews, the forms, the questions—they forced Anthony to face fears he'd buried. But each step forward, each obstacle they crossed, chipped away at his doubts. Caroline's strength steadied him, her resolve a quiet flame he hadn't realized he needed.

And as they moved forward, he began to believe, just maybe, that he could become the father he'd never thought he could be.

Anthony sat in the familiar and slightly uncomfortable chair across from Dr. Everett's desk. Typically, Dr E's office was a sanctuary of predictable routine and professional chatter, but it was unconventionally shut off for most of the day. Anthony felt a surge of foreboding when he was called in for a closed-door conversation. His boss, who's usually composed and freewheeling, was a bundle of nerves. He was fidgeting with papers he didn't seem interested in reading while avoiding eye contact like a teenager with a guilty conscience.

Dr. Everett eventually sighed with a sound that seemed to carry the weight of the world, or at least the weight of a conversation he clearly wanted to avoid. He tapped the desk lightly which was a prelude to the inevitable. "Anthony," he began as his voice walked a tightrope between professional and awkward, "I want you to know, this is a conversation I don't want to have... and never want to again for that matter."

Anthony's stomach lurched into a slow and dreadful somersault. "Is everything alright? You're making me nervous." His voice was steady, but his insides felt like they were being wrung out.

Dr. Everett gave him a brief glance. His face was already tinged with discomfort, as if he were about to sever something that wouldn't grow back. "We've had... um, we've had a few complaints. And I've gotta be honest, when I first heard them, I was skeptical. In fact, I was looking around for a candid camera. Unfortunately, much to my dismay, this is all too real."

"Complaints?" Anthony repeated, feeling his brain freeze. His professionalism had never been in question before. His mind raced through the possibilities. "Complaints about what?"

Dr. Everett shifted uncomfortably, like a man forced to deliver news no one should ever have to hear. "Yes, uh, it's, uh, a very sensitive subject. Like I was saying, I didn't believe it at first. I didn't even bother to investigate. But, after hearing from a few patients... well, I felt I had to observe for myself. It's something that I'll never be able to unsee."

Anthony's palms grew clammy as he clinched up. "What did you see?" he asked. His voice edged with the kind of dread reserved for hearing the last nail being hammered into a coffin.

Dr. Everett's face grew flushed like an embarrassed schoolboy. He cleared his throat. "There's been... an issue. A pattern, actually. The complaints all pointed to, well... inappropriate arousal."

Anthony's face turned ghostly pale, as if every drop of blood had been called elsewhere. Arousal? This had to be some kind of nightmare. His heart was pounding like it wanted to jump out and make a run for it.

Dr. Everett leaned forward, his voice dropped to a conspiratorial whisper, as if the walls might develop ears at any moment. "Look, I initially doubted it. I mean, the first complaint was from Edith, a sixty-year-old patient, for crying out loud. I thought, surely she's mistaken, but then we had another... and another. And when I watched a few of your sessions, I... I saw it, and I'll forever be traumatized by it. This is... I never thought I'd be in this position as a manager. It's just so strange and uncomfortable."

Anthony wanted to sink into the floor and vanish into some alternate reality where his boss wasn't sitting here talking about "inappropriate arousal." He was reliving the moment Mark Fields caught him in that bathroom stall all over again. "What... exactly did you see?" he managed to ask, knowing full well he didn't want to hear the answer.

"Your boy scout pitched a tent in your exercise pants," Dr. Everett stammered, his face now resembling a ripe tomato. "In your... genital area. It wasn't as pronounced as I would have expected, but it was... noticeable."

Anthony slumped back in his chair while his mind spun. He hadn't realized anyone could notice. He didn't even know it was happening most of the time. The line between professional and personal had blurred in the worst possible way. He always tried to stay focused, but the closeness, the touch, the groans of agony the women made were somehow interpreted as pleasure. And truth be told, it was exciting to experience for once. But how could he explain that?

"I... I didn't mean for it to happen," Anthony said, barely above a whisper. "I swear, it wasn't intentional."

Dr. Everett sighed again while leaning back in his chair. He was clearly relieved the words were finally out. "I believe you, Anthony. I do. However, this isn't something we can overlook. Patients need to feel safe, both physically and emotionally. Even if it's subconscious, it's just not appropriate in this setting."

Anthony's head dropped as the weight of his failure settled on his shoulders like a heavy coat. He'd lost control over the one thing that made him feel relevant. "So, what happens now?"

Dr. Everett hesitated and rubbed his temples as though he had a massive headache. "Anthony, I'm afraid we have no choice but to let you go. We can't risk the clinic's reputation, and we certainly can't let this continue. It's not that I don't feel for you, but... you can't stay in this job."

Anthony nodded, unable to speak. He knew this was coming but hearing it out loud made it feel like the world was falling in on him.

"I'm sorry, Anthony," Dr. Everett added, standing up. "You're a talented therapist, but this isn't something we can just overlook or accommodate. I'm sure you'll find something better suited for you. Just... not with patients."

Anthony's numb hand shook Dr. Everett's. The conversation replayed in his mind as he walked out of the clinic for the last time. He felt like a man adrift. He was untethered from the only thing that had given his life structure. And now he had to go home and tell Caroline.

The smell of baking greeted him as he stepped into the apartment, but it did nothing to soothe the anxiety swirling in his gut. Caroline looked up from her recipe book and greeted him with a smile.

"Hey, you're home early!" she said. Her voice was light and oblivious to the storm that was about to hit.

Anthony stood in the doorway with dread coursing through his veins. "We need to talk," he said, with a thick voice.

Caroline's smile faded as concern washed over her face. "What's wrong?"

Anthony swallowed hard while the bitter truth rose in his throat like bile. "I lost my job."

Her brow furrowed in confusion. "Wait, what? Why?"

Anthony hesitated; he was unsure how to frame the disaster without making it sound worse than it already was. "There were… complaints. Some of the patients thought I was… getting aroused during their sessions."

Caroline's eyes widened in shock. "What?"

Ashamed, Anthony looked down at the floor. "It wasn't intentional. It just… happened."

Still reeling from the shock, she took a step back as her confusion turned into disbelief. "You were getting aroused by your patients?"

"I didn't mean for it to happen, Caroline," Anthony pleaded. "It's just… the nature of… I guess I didn't handle it well."

Her lips buttoned up. "And you didn't think to tell me? You didn't think about stopping? You're a pervert."

"I didn't even realize it was a problem until it was too late," he said weakly. "I swear, I wasn't trying to do anything wrong."

Caroline's expression hardened while anger simmered beneath the surface. "So, what happens now? What about your career? What are we supposed to do?"

Anthony shook his head and felt utterly lost. "I don't know. I'll find another job."

Caroline's face grew wicked, and her words were biting. "I married a Physical Therapist, not some-other job."

"Caroline, I—"

"I thought I was marrying someone with his life together. Someone with a plan. But you can't keep a job or give me children, and now learning that you're getting aroused by other women while you're supposed to be working? What kind of husband are you?"

Her words cut through him, but he was too stunned to respond.

Tears welled in her eyes as she shook her head. "I've been unhappy since our vows. You treat me like I belong to you and not the partner I am meant to be. I don't want this anymore, Anthony. I've spent the last year feeling trapped. You're already going bald, you give me no pleasure, you seek other women, and you can't get me pregnant, and you don't love me nor want a family."

"I promise, I'll work on it," Anthony begged. "I do love you. We'll adopt, I'll find another job, I'll do whatever it takes…"

"No," Caroline said firmly, cutting him off. "I'm done. I'm keeping the ring and I'm leaving. I've been planning on how to leave you for some time, and the right time is now."

With that, she walked to their bedroom, stuffed her suitcase from under the bed, and walked out. Abruptly, Anthony was left standing alone in their apartment. His entire world crumbled around him in an instant that afternoon.

Chapter 11: Reinventing Himself

Anthony Pollock sat in his lonely apartment, stacks of classifieds spread before him like a bleak reminder of his options, or lack of them. The ink from the pages smudged his fingers, staining them as he scanned the want ads, hunting for any possible lifeline. Each listing he circled led nowhere. Each promising ad was crossed out, dead ends stacking up like tombstones. The truth gnawed at him: Boston's clinics had blacklisted him. He could still feel the weight of those final moments with Dr. Everett, the disgust in his voice, the way he'd dismissed Anthony as though he were contagious.

He leaned back and rubbed his scalp, feeling bare skin where his hair had begun to recede. It seemed even his body was abandoning him. The radio droned in the background, a half-hearted comfort against the silence closing in. He'd tried everything: calls to old contacts, visits to employment agencies. Every lead fizzled the moment questions about his past arose. His reputation was ruined.

A flash of memory hit him, an old conversation from his Harvard days with a classmate who had mentioned working in schools. She chose an educational setting rather than a clinical one. "For people who can't hack it in a real environment," he'd thought at the time, dismissing the idea as beneath him. But now, with the specter of clinical work behind him, the idea of teaching others instead of working hands-on started to appeal. He wasn't likely to have another chance at clinical work, not after what happened.

With just a flicker of hope, he flipped through a random out-of-state classified. Then his eye caught something: School-Based Physical Therapist Needed. The ad was buried between listings for truck drivers and warehouse workers. It looked somewhat hopeful. The position wasn't in Boston; it was a small town out west. The salary was low, laughable even. But that one line stood out like a flare against a dark sky: Not a clinical position. License required. Start immediately.

Anthony's heart started racing. He wouldn't have to work directly with patients, no risk of the past following him, no threat of old mistakes creeping in. The role described something close to a consultant's job. No touch, no personal space to invade, just oversight. He circled the ad in red, picked up the phone, and dialed the number. The receiver felt warm and light in his hand.

After a few rings, a friendly voice answered. "Mountain View Regional Education Bureau, how may I help you?"

Anthony cleared his throat, his words coming out rough. "Yes, I'm calling about the Physical Therapist position listed in the paper."

The woman transferred him, and he soon found himself speaking to the Specialized Student Care Director, Margaret Sanders. She launched into the job details eagerly, her voice animated with the kind of hope he hadn't heard in weeks.

"We've struggled to find a qualified candidate," she admitted, sounding both exhausted and relieved. "We're a small bureau, and, well, it's not exactly the most glamorous role. We need someone who can train our teachers to help students with basic physical needs: simple exercises, positioning, that sort of thing. You wouldn't be working directly with the students. Mostly, you'd just teach the staff."

Anthony held the phone tighter. This was it. The opened door he'd been desperate for. "I have experience and am licensed," he said, trying to inject some confidence into his voice. "I'd be more than capable of training others."

Margaret sounded even more enthusiastic. "Oh, that's wonderful! Someone with your background would be perfect. Could you come for an interview?"

Anthony hesitated. The travel would eat up the last of his savings, and he didn't have much left after his dismissal. "Actually," he began carefully, "I'm out of state right now. Could we do the interview over the phone?"

She paused, and he held his breath. "You know," she said finally, "that could work. We're in a bit of a bind, and you sound like you have just the experience we need. Let's go ahead and do it over the phone."

The interview itself was brief, almost unsettlingly easy. Margaret was less concerned with specifics and more focused on finding someone who would simply say yes. She didn't probe much, didn't ask about his former job. The whole time, Anthony kept waiting for the other shoe to drop, for some question that would shatter the fragile hope he felt. But by the end, Margaret was offering him the job on the spot.

"It's a teacher's salary," she warned, her tone apologetic. "Nothing too high, but the cost of living's low out here. We mostly need you to train staff and check in every so often. You'll have plenty of flexibility to set your own schedule."

Anthony agreed, a wave of relief so heavy it nearly buckled him. The job wasn't perfect. The pay was barely enough to scrape by, and the isolation of some small town he'd never heard of hardly felt like a step up. But it was an escape. A fresh start. He could dodge the clinical scrutiny, the watching eyes, and all the risks that had haunted him. He could disappear into a place where his past couldn't reach him.

Within two weeks, he'd packed up his apartment, sold what couldn't fit in his car, and set off for the West. He even bought himself a derby hat for the drive, as if donning a new uniform could make the transformation complete. As the crowded streets of Boston gave way to rolling hills and open plains, he felt a strange, exhilarating sense of freedom. The failures, the shame, the specter of his marriage, they all faded into the rearview mirror, swallowed up by miles of open road.

When he finally reached his destination, the town was even smaller and more rural than he had imagined. The population barely crested 10,000, mostly farmers and ranchers, with a main street that looked like it hadn't seen a fresh coat of paint in decades. The Mountain View Regional Education Bureau office sat in a rundown brick building on the edge of town, surrounded by range land, with the mountains looming in the distance like silent sentries.

Margaret Sanders met him at the entrance. Her silver hair was pulled back in a neat bun, and she had a firm handshake. Her no-nonsense attitude came through immediately. It was a quality he hadn't expected in someone out here, but it set him at ease.

"We're glad to have you," she said, leading him into the office. "Finding someone willing to take on this role has been a real challenge. I think you'll fit in just fine."

"Thank you," he replied. "I'm looking forward to getting started."

Margaret handed him a thick packet. "Here's everything you need to know. We serve six school districts, so you'll rotate between them. Mostly, you'll train the staff on handling physical therapy exercises. You won't need to do hands-on work unless there's an emergency or a complicated case. We leave the day-to-day care to the teachers and aides."

As she spoke, Anthony's shoulder tension ebbed. The job was everything he'd hoped for: low pressure, minimal oversight, and a complete lack of direct patient contact. No one was breathing down his neck. No one watching for the faintest hint of impropriety. He could drift through the schools, give the teachers basic instructions, check in every so often, and keep his distance. The idea of such freedom felt almost surreal.

Margaret continued, unaware of his relief. "I feel like I need to reiterate that this job, it's a teacher's salary, and the work can get a little monotonous, but it's steady. You'll have a set schedule but plenty of freedom with it. Are you sure this is what you want?"

"Oh yes, I am sure!" Anthony thanked her, grateful beyond words. This job didn't demand much from him, and no one here seemed eager to ask questions. He really wasn't in a position to ask for more than that. For the first time in months, his worries dissolved into tranquility.

Over the next few days, Anthony settled into his main street apartment, a modest place with an unremarkable view of the town's primary commerce strip. It wasn't the life he'd imagined for himself back at Harvard, but it was safe, and he could live with that.

The town, the job, the simplicity of it, maybe this small-town life would work out. Maybe, finally, he'd found a place where he could just exist, a place where failure couldn't find him.

It wasn't much. But for now, it was a win.

Chapter 12: The Future's Dawn

Anthony stood in the lobby of the Mountain View Regional Education Bureau office, feeling a strange mixture of nerves and anticipation. This was a new world, working in a small, rural district, far from the prestige he'd once imagined for himself. But, after all he's been through, his new life is a blessing. He needed a fresh start, and this job, as unglamorous as it was, might just be his ticket to some stability.

The day began when the lobby door creaked open and in walked Mike, the other physical therapist on staff. Mike looked like someone who had long since stopped pretending to care too much about his job. He was a scruffy man in his mid-forties, dressed in jeans and a button-down shirt, with a spark of humor in his eyes that made Anthony feel welcome.

"You must be Anthony," Mike said, offering a lazy handshake. "I'm Mike. Looks like I'm your guide to this glorious institution."

"Yes, that is me," Anthony replied, shaking his hand. "Good to meet you."

"Yeah, well, let's get this over with," Mike said, turning to lead Anthony down the hall. "I'll give you the grand tour. It won't take long." They started down a narrow corridor lined with outdated motivational posters and mismatched furniture. Mike launched into his spiel with a mix of dry humor and weary resignation.

"So, our Mountain View REB, or just bureau for short," Mike began, gesturing as they walked. "We've been around since the '70s. The school districts around here don't want to manage all the medical services for kids with special needs, so they pooled their resources and created us. We handle everything they don't know how to deal with:

physical therapy, speech therapy, occupational therapy, all that good stuff."

Anthony nodded, taking it in. "Makes sense."

"Yeah, it does make sense," Mike said with a smirk. "Until you realize that no one in charge here has any idea what we do either. All the higher-ups here, they're former teachers and school administrators. They too have no medical background. So, they just trust us to handle it. We're the professionals, after all."

Anthony chuckled at Mike's dry tone. "There's not a lot of oversight?"

Mike shook his head. "Not really. If the paperwork's in order and the kids are getting what they need, at least what we say they need, nobody asks too many questions. You'll be writing up reports, figuring out how much therapy each student needs, and making sure it happens. But no one's going to be checking on you every five minutes."

As they reached a small break room, Mike grabbed a cup of coffee and leaned against the counter, eyeing Anthony with a half-smile. "You know, it's funny. In most other countries, medical stuff stays in hospitals. But here, thanks to the Education for All Handicapped Children Act of 1975, schools are responsible for providing everything from therapy to transportation. The costs add up fast. That's why education costs so much more here compared to other countries, at least on a per student basis."

Anthony raised an eyebrow. "School Districts are paying for all of this?"

"Yup," Mike replied. "You've got kids who need special buses, extra staff, sometimes entire classrooms just for them. All that comes from the school budget. And the bureau manages the therapists and specialists, so the schools don't have to deal with it directly. We're their special education saviors."

Mike took a sip of his coffee, grinning. "The best part? We're pretty much left to our own devices. You pop into a school, show the staff how to help the kids with their exercises, and that's it. No one's looking over your shoulder. Plus, our dress code is pretty casual."

Anthony felt a wave of relief. This was exactly what he needed, a minimum pressure job where he could operate without constant supervision. After everything that had happened in Boston, this was sounding better and better.

"Sounds pretty rad," Anthony admitted, trying not to sound too eager.

Mike chuckled. "Yeah, it's a rad gig if you're not looking for fame or fortune. Just steady work, no drama. You'll be treated well just as long as you keep the paperwork neat."

When Anthony finally settled into his new office, he felt good. This job wasn't what he'd once dreamed of, but it was stable, and for now, that was comforting.

After he completed his first day on the job, Anthony sat in his small apartment, reliving the events of the day. It had gone better than he expected; Mike's laid-back attitude and the lack of oversight made him feel like he'd found a soft landing. But one thing still nagged at him. He hadn't told his father about his divorce, the move, or the new job.

He sighed, picked up the phone, and dialed. The rotary phone clicked as he turned the dial, and after a few rings, Barton's familiar, clipped voice answered.

"Yes?"

"Hello father," Anthony said, trying to sound steady. "I just wanted to let you know that I got divorced and moved out west. I took a job with the Mountain View Regional Educational Bureau."

There was a pause, and Anthony waited, unsure what to expect. Barton had always been a tough nut to crack, distant, cold, always focused on his own ambitions, but Anthony still harbored a faint hope that maybe this time his father might be proud of him for finding steady work, for rebuilding his life.

"Oh?" Barton replied, his voice was neutral not dismissive, which was a nice change. "What's this job?"

Anthony's heart lifted a bit. Maybe Barton was interested.

"I'm working with schools as a consultant," Anthony explained. "Helping students with physical therapy. The bureau handles much of the special education services for the surrounding school districts. It's actually pretty interesting. Schools here can't just focus on education. They must provide medical services for students with disabilities while at school. Things like physical therapy, speech therapy, even transportation. There's a lot more going on than just teaching."

Another pause left Anthony feeling a flicker of hope. Hopefully Barton will acknowledge the significance of the job, the responsibility that came with it.

"Schools are paying for student's medical services?" Barton asked, his tone still neutral, but now with a trace of curiosity.

"Yeah," Anthony replied. "That's why education costs so much in the U.S. compared to other countries. Schools are responsible for all these additional services. Districts pay us to make sure the kids get what they need."

There was a long silence at the other end of the line, as Anthony bathed in anticipation. Was Barton actually impressed? Maybe, just maybe, his father was proud of him for finding something steady, something important.

"Interesting," Barton finally said, his voice thoughtful. "I didn't realize schools had so many costs that weren't academic in nature."

Anthony felt a surge of happiness. His father was interested. He wanted to hear more about the job. He started to believe Barton saw the value in what he was doing after all.

In reality, Barton wasn't proud of his son's new career or cared that he is now divorced, nor was he impressed with Anthony's role in the education system. Barton was filing away the information, learning about the budget burdens of the education system, taking note of the fact that schools were handling medical care on the taxpayers' dime. He wasn't interested in the massive benefit of having a literate society that public schools provide. It was just another piece of data for him to use when the time came, another potential political tool to distract voters or stir up controversy where one shouldn't exist.

"Well, I just wanted to let you know," Anthony said, his voice still hopeful. "It's a good job, and I'm settling in."

"Right," Barton replied, his tone distant again. "I wish you the best of luck."

Anthony hung up the phone, feeling both relieved and a little hollow. He had hoped, for just a moment, that his father could muster the emotional fortitude to be proud of him. That perhaps Barton's interest in the job meant something more than it did. But deep down, Anthony worried he didn't impress his father. It's something Anthony has constantly fallen short of. Barton wasn't proud of his work or his new life. He was just going through the motions, trying to figure out what parts of his life his father can use for bragging rights.

Anthony sighed and leaned back into his chair, staring out the window at the darkening sky. Even if it wasn't what he'd once dreamed of, he's found stability in his new job. His father's approval may never come. But for now, he had a new beginning, and he was thankful for that.

Chapter 13: The Gamble

Anthony, surrounded by friends, sat in his regular spot at his local tavern with the familiar sight of beer in his hand. The chatter of his colleagues filled the air with typical work-place politics. He was established, and his life, for the most part, was comfortable. He had carved out a place for himself at the bureau. He was well-liked by coworkers and supervisors. They saw him as intelligent, sincere, warm, well-educated, and dependable. He was a regular at the local trivia nights, where his vast knowledge of obscure facts, honed from years of reading and studying Barton's book, made him a local legend.

Everyone wanted him on their trivia team. They'd marvel at his ability to recall random facts, and the tales he'd casually drop every now and then, that he had sung at Carnegie Hall, or tales of Harvard, never failed to impress. His father, Barton, had planted that seed in his head all those years ago, and Anthony still enjoyed the reactions it brought. Even though it wasn't the whole truth, it was enough to keep his status as a mysterious, gifted man intact.

On the outside, Anthony's life was good. He had friends, he had a steady job, and in a rural area like this, he had built a reputation as someone who knew how to live. But beneath the surface, there was worry.

Despite his popularity, Anthony remained single over the last two decades, avoiding romantic relationships like the plague. He stuck with pornography as his outlet, nervous that if he got too close to someone, they'd find out about his condition and insecurities. He was afraid they'd learn he was, in fact, a deeply flawed man, whose accomplishments are more of a facade. To this day, he has unresolved fears about intimacy, vulnerability, and the inability to pleasure a woman.

His looks had changed too. Over the years, male pattern baldness crept in, leaving him bald under his consistently worn derby hat. To throw people off the scent of his hair loss, he grew a ponytail, which somehow made him feel hip, even though he just looked like a short bald guy with a compensating ponytail. He hoped people would see the ponytail and cap and assume he had a full head of hair... it wasn't so, but no one told him any different.

As much as he enjoyed his social life, there was a problem he would have to face, a problem he couldn't ignore forever. The field of physical therapy was changing. When Anthony graduated, a bachelor's degree was all that was required to practice in his field. He had been grandfathered in when the profession transitioned to requiring a master's degree a few years ago. But now, the stakes were even higher. In just a few years, a doctorate would be required for all physical therapists, no exceptions, no grandfathering in.

Anthony understood he had no chance of getting a doctorate in physical therapy. He had barely escaped his bachelor's program, and that was so long ago. Going back to school now, for something as grueling as a doctorate in physical therapy, was simply out of the question. His work at the bureau wasn't traditional hands-on therapy, so he didn't have the practical experience to keep him current. The thought of enrolling in an intense academic program filled him with dread.

Luckily there was a possible alternative. Recently, the Mountain View REB introduced a program offering to pay for employees to earn a continuing degree if their license required more education. It was designed to support staff who require advanced degrees to continue practicing. However, the program had a loophole. It didn't specify that the advanced degree had to be in the employee's specific field of specialty, just if a higher degree was necessary. This loophole sparked an idea in Anthony's mind.

Instead of going back to school for physical therapy, a feat he knew he couldn't manage, he would apply for a doctorate in education. It would be easier, and if he completed it, it would position him for a promotion. His boss at the bureau was set to retire in a few years, and with a doctorate in education, Anthony could potentially step into a leadership role. He'd be able to keep his job, even get a raise, and avoid the crushing demands to remain a physical therapist.

His plan had risks and there were logistical challenges too. The internet was still in its infancy, so he couldn't learn from home, and doctorate programs in his region were nonexistent. However, one option did exist for rural students. Anthony could attend classes at the local community college's remote learning center, which had video conferencing capabilities, and utilize the mail to turn in assignments. It wasn't ideal, but it was the only way to pursue this doctorate and keep his job. But, what if his boss didn't retire before the Physical Therapy requirement took effect, or she did but he wasn't selected to replace her? These complications weighed heavy, but what else was he to do but make the gamble.

Anthony spread the paperwork across his small dining table. The doctorate program wasn't from a prestigious university, but that didn't matter. A doctorate was a doctorate, and with his career on the line, he couldn't afford to be picky.

He filled out the forms carefully, writing about his commitment to education, his desire to contribute more to the bureau, and his hopes of advancing in the field. He couldn't exactly tell the truth, that this was a gamble to keep his job, but he didn't feel too bad about bending the narrative. After all, he had come to care about the people he worked with, the students who benefited from the services provided, and the friends he had made along the way. It wasn't all a lie.

Once the forms were filled out, he placed them in a large envelope and sealed it. He'd mail it in the morning, and after that, the waiting game would begin.

Weeks passed, and Anthony settled back into his routine. He still visited schools, guided the staff, and kept up appearances as the friendly and gifted guy everyone liked. The looming changes in the physical therapy field were always in the back of his mind, but he tried to push them aside as best he could. He'd taken every step he could to secure his future, now he just had to hope the bureau would approve his application if accepted.

One evening, after a round of trivia, his colleagues brought up the doctorate requirement in casual conversation. "You worried about that doctorate thing, Anthony?" his friend asked, leaning back in his chair. "You've been here for a while. Think you're gonna go back to school?"

Anthony smiled, keeping his tone light. "I've got a plan," he said, taking a sip of his drink. "Might not be what you expect, but I've got something in the works."

His friend raised an eyebrow but didn't press. "Well, you're the smartest guy here so you'll figure it out."

Anthony chuckled along with the others, but inside, he felt the seriousness of the gamble he'd taken. If this doctorate in education plan worked, he could ride the wave of changes and maybe even climb the career ladder. If it didn't...he didn't want to think about that.

He got the news a few weeks later. His application had been accepted. He was officially enrolled in the education doctorate program. His classes would start soon. He'd spend his evenings at the community college's remote learning center, attending lectures through video conferencing. It wasn't glamorous, but it was his way forward.

As he left the bar that night, Anthony felt the comforting weight of his derby hat as he adjusted it on his head, the brim casting a shadow over his eyes. He walked through the quiet, dark streets of the town he had come to call home, each step slow and measured. The faces and laughter from the bar lingered in his mind, the casual warmth of friends who saw him as the clever, reliable Anthony Pollock, a man who always had a quip and a trivia answer, a man who belonged.

But he knew better. He felt the stress and anxiety that had taken up permanent residence in his thoughts. Beneath his easygoing smile, beneath his carefully crafted tales of Carnegie Hall and Harvard lay the creeping worry of how long he could keep up this charade. Tonight, he assured his friends he had "something in the works," a plan to deal with the new Physical Therapist requirements. They had laughed, patted his shoulder, and trusted him, as they always did. But what would they think if they knew the truth? That he was sidestepping the profession he'd been grandfathered into? That his new graduate degree wouldn't be in physical therapy but in education, an easier route he'd chosen out of desperation?

He could almost hear the scoffs, the letdowns that would ripple through his small circle. Anthony walked faster, as if to outrun the questions swirling in his mind. He'd taken a gamble, a big one. His entire career now hinged on this plan. If the bureau didn't approve of his degree or if his boss delayed retirement, everything could fall apart. He'd be left exposed, his clever maneuvers reduced to nothing more than another failed scheme.

The night air was cool, and a breeze swept through the empty street, rustling leaves and lifting the brim of his hat. He pulled it down firmly, clinging to the sense of control it gave him. This doctorate wasn't what he'd once imagined for himself, and it wasn't anything that could make his father proud. But it was survival, plain and simple. He could live with that.

Anthony glanced up, the stars spread wide above him, distant and unreachable. He forced a smile, a small reassurance for himself, as if that could make the gamble feel certain. But doubt lingered, slipping through the cracks he tried to seal tight. His future rested on luck and timing; forces he couldn't control. He committed to this path, and he would see it through, but the seas ahead looked rough.

When he finally reached his apartment door, he paused, took a deep breath, and let the familiar smell of the old building ground him. The future waited, uncertain and distant. And as he turned his key in the lock, he knew he'd bought himself time—but just how much, he couldn't say.

Chapter 14: Completing the Circle

Anthony sat in the small, dimly lit room at the community college's remote learning center, staring at the flickering video screen in front of him. The doctorate program he had enrolled in was, frankly, a joke. It wasn't affiliated with a prestigious university; it was barely a legitimate institution at all. The coursework was minimal, and the assignments felt more like busy work than anything meaningful. It was the kind of place where anyone could buy their degree if they just kept showing up and doing the bare minimum.

This arrangement was fine with Anthony. He didn't need a rigorous education. All he needed was the piece of paper that would allow him advancement with the Mountain View REB, once his boss retired. A postgraduate degree, no matter how flimsy the institution, still carried tremendous weight. He wouldn't have to worry about the looming physical therapy requirements. It wasn't the noble road, but it was the smart one. However, what Anthony hadn't expected was to meet someone like Cynthia.

Cynthia ran the community college distance learning program. From the moment Anthony met her, there was something about her that intrigued him. She was articulate and well-kept, always dressed in neat, understated professional attire that complimented her polished demeanor. She had a sharp wit, a quiet elegance, and a kind of unspoken strength that drew Anthony in.

She was about ten years older than Anthony, but that didn't bother him. Cynthia had lived a life that mirrored his in ways he hadn't expected.

She had been married once too, but it ended after she had undergone an emergency hysterectomy. Her husband at the time, who had wanted children more than anything, couldn't accept that her condition would disqualify his opportunity. He refused the idea of adoption, and eventually, their marriage unraveled.

For Anthony, that story hit close to home. He too couldn't sire a child. His condition kept his sperm count far too low, a fact that had haunted him since his brief, failed marriage. But unlike Cynthia's ex-husband, Anthony had always considered being a parent more of a burden than a necessity. Still, the rejection Cynthia experienced struck a chord.

They started out as friends. At first, it was simple conversations between classes, small talk about the absurdity of the doctorate program or light banter about life in the small town. But, as time went on, their friendship deepened. Cynthia was witty and fun, but she carried herself with a sense of grace and class that made Anthony feel comfortable in her presence. She accepted him without judgment, something Anthony had rarely experienced in his life.

Over time, that friendship blossomed into something more. There was a tenderness between them, an unspoken understanding of each other's insecurities. Anthony had long avoided relationships, afraid that if anyone got too close, they'd discover the truth about him, his past, his fears, and his *"Tiny Tony"* that's responsible for his inability to have children. But with Cynthia, there was no need to hide.

She, too, had her fears. After her marriage ended, she had lived with the quiet fear of being abandoned again, of letting someone in only to have them walk away when she needed them most. But with Anthony, there was none of that. They both knew children were not in their future, and that was firm reality for both of them.

Their relationship didn't follow the traditional trajectory. It wasn't the passionate whirlwind romance Anthony had once imagined, but something deeper, built on companionship, trust, and mutual understanding. Cynthia was older, and Anthony knew she wasn't the "catch" that some might expect. But her company, her acceptance, and the quiet life they built together meant more to him than he had realized.

Still, the age difference didn't go unnoticed by others. People at the community college and the bureau speculated. Some wondered if Anthony was using Cynthia to avoid deeper emotional connections, while others, who had assumed Anthony was gay, after his years of remaining a bachelor, were confused by what appeared to others as a sudden relationship. The whispers didn't bother them; both had lived through too much to care about what others were thinking.

One evening, after Anthony had finished another lackluster video lecture, they sat together at Cynthia's home, sharing a bottle of wine. The warmth between them was familiar now, and they talked about their future.

"Do you ever think about getting married again?" Cynthia asked, her voice soft but serious. Anthony hesitated, swirling his wine. He was nervous and excited about where the conversation was going. "I guess I do," he said quietly. "I just didn't think it would happen like this."

Cynthia smiled. Her eyes filled with understanding. "Does it bother you? The way people talk? The age difference?" He shook his head. "No. It used to, but not anymore. We've both been through enough to know what's important. I don't care what anyone else thinks."

Her smile deepened, and she reached out to take his hand. "Good. Because I was thinking... we could make this official. Quietly. No big wedding. Just us."

Anthony squeezed her hand, feeling a sense of peace washing over him. It wasn't the life he had envisioned when he was younger, but it was real, and it was theirs. "Yeah," he said softly. "I think I'd like that."

A few weeks later, they eloped in a quiet ceremony, far from the judgmental eyes of their colleagues and friends. There were no elaborate plans, no guest lists or fanfare, just the two of them, committing to each other without the need for anyone's approval.

Anthony's friends at the bureau were surprised by the news, especially those who had long assumed he was into men. The age difference and the elopement only fueled the gossip, but Anthony didn't care. For the first time in his life, he found something genuine, something that didn't require him to hide or pretend.

As for the doctorate program, Anthony continued his classes, knowing that soon he would have the degree he needed. The program remained laughably easy, and while the work wasn't challenging, he knew it would give him what he needed, his title of "Dr. Anthony Pollock" and the chance to move into a higher-paying administrative role at the bureau. No one would care how he'd gotten the degree, only that he had it.

Between his new marriage and his soon-to-be professional capital, Anthony found a way to reconcile his past with his future. It wasn't perfect, but it was his. And after everything he had been through, his path forward was illuminated with optimism.

Chapter 15: Ascending

Anthony stood in front of his bathroom mirror, adjusting his tie for what felt like the hundredth time. His heart thumping as he took in his reflection, both pleased and unsure. The new haircut—professional short—felt sharp, but he missed the symbolism of his old ponytail. He could almost hear Barton in his head, telling him to "look the part." Today, he did. After many years as a physical therapist for the bureau, he finally had the chance to step out of the shadows and into a position of real authority: Specialized Student Care Director.

This was his moment. His boss was finally retiring, and his own eligibility to stay on as a physical therapist was nearing its end. But that didn't matter anymore. His hastily earned doctorate in education, the one he'd completed remotely through a less-than-rigorous program, would keep him from slipping off the professional radar. With a title like Director, he would escape the diminishing role of therapist and instead oversee the very services he had spent years providing, with a bigger salary and a private office. As director, he'd be something; he'd be someone. He needed this.

He wasn't the only candidate, of course. Some classroom teachers were competing for the position, eager to move into administration. Good educators, each of them, but they lacked the specific experience he knew set him apart. Bureau services demanded a unique blend of therapy, medical services, and individualized plans that few understood as he did. This was his edge.

As he tightened his tie one last time, a smile crept over his face. Over his career, he played his part well. He built the right relationships, fostered his image, won colleagues' respect as "the smartest guy around"—helped, in no small part, by his trivia prowess and the half-truth of his "Harvard" background. He was a local legend in the bureau's trivia nights: the man with a wealth of random facts who sang at Carnegie Hall. In his own way, he'd become admired. But this... this was bigger than a trivia contest. It was his chance to prove, finally, that he was more than Barton's son, more than the role he'd been stuck in all these years.

The interview itself went as smoothly as he'd hoped. He knew everyone on the committee, having worked alongside them since his early days. He felt their eyes on him, trusted their nods and faint smiles. They asked him the typical questions: his vision for special education, his plans to support staff and students, his approach to managing budgets. He answered easily, pulling from his years of experience and his knowledge of physical therapy. Special education wasn't just about academics; it required an understanding of medical needs and the ability to balance complex care with educational goals. This, he told them, was where he shined.

The committee looked impressed. They clearly agreed as he spoke about the bureau's unique role in providing services that other schools couldn't manage on their own. He could feel their approval, their recognition of his worth. By the time he walked out, he'd felt relief flooding him, the weight of years of work lifting. He'd done it; he'd shown them he was capable, smart, and prepared.

The very next day, the call came. He was chosen as the new Specialized Student Care Director. Sitting in his new office, Anthony let the sense of victory wash over him. He had gone from someone unhirable in Boston, to a physical therapist skirting the edge of career oblivion, to the director of an entire department. The timing could not have been better, nor the stakes higher. His flimsy doctorate had opened a door to heights he'd barely dared imagine before enrolling.

His mind went to the pay bump, the recognition, the sense of finally being able to hold his head high. He'd become the success he'd told everyone he was. Years of staying under the radar, of building his reputation as "the Harvard man" and "trivia king," had finally led to something real. In those early days, he hadn't known exactly what he was building, but now he saw the shape of it—a position, a career, a place to belong. He had something concrete to show for his efforts.

His colleagues, relieved by his appointment, seemed comforted that Anthony didn't plan to shake things up. He had no interest in raising expectations or pushing for new programs. He preferred the status quo, the relaxed culture of the bureau that had served him so well. No need to upset a system that worked just fine as it was.

Instead, he turned his focus outward, nurturing relationships with the school districts that funded the bureau's programs. Without their support, his department would falter, and he needed their investments secure. They relied on the bureau to handle students' medical and therapeutic needs, and he needed them to rely on him. He started attending their meetings, smoothing over concerns, ensuring communication stayed open. The schmoozing, the gentle reassurance, the art of giving people just enough to feel satisfied, it played to his strengths. Reading people, giving them what they wanted without overpromising, was his comfort zone. And the extra pay didn't hurt.

As he settled into his new position, his thoughts turned to Barton. He had become his own success, but his father's shadow still lingered in the back of his mind. Barton Pollock, a man who had spent his life chasing power, had always been a looming figure. Growing up, Anthony had chased that shadow, had done whatever he could to feel worthy of the name Pollock. He wondered if Barton had always judged him for taking a government job, for not becoming something bigger. But maybe, just maybe, this promotion could finally change that. His father had spent years teaching him that power defined a man's worth, and now, Anthony was finally wielding it himself.

As he gazed out of his office window, a mix of nerves and excitement grew inside him. He grabbed his phone and dialed Barton's number.

The phone rang twice before his father's voice cut through, crisp, businesslike as ever. "Barton Pollock."

Anthony cleared his throat. "Dad, I've got news. I'm the new Director of Specialized Student Care. It's a big step for me."

There was a brief pause, then Barton's voice shifted, lit with real enthusiasm, but not for his son. "That's great, son," he said quickly, his words barely concealing his true excitement. "But listen, something big just happened. A deal's been struck between a powerful gossip media mogul and our top campaign strategist to create a 24-hour news channel. Do you understand what this means? We're not just setting a narrative anymore; we'll be controlling the reality for millions viewers."

Anthony felt his stomach sink as his father's voice filled with fervor. "That sounds...important," he managed.

"Oh, it's more than important," Barton continued, almost breathless with excitement. "We're talking about manipulation on a mass scale, son. It's one thing to shape opinions, but to control their beliefs? To make them believe whatever we say, regardless of the facts? It's pure genius. We're about to create a loyal voting base that trusts only us—no science, no media, no outside information. They'll believe that every system out there is fraudulent, except for us. We'll be the only trusted source."

Anthony forced himself to laugh, though it felt strained. "That's...quite a feat."

Barton laughed, delighted. "It's brilliant! We're going to make them believe that if we say the sun is shining, it must be our doing, and if it's raining, it's the fault of some weatherman who's been lying to them all along. They'll trust only us, and that's the power we've been working for. This is how you change the world, Anthony. This is the future of our country."

Anthony gripped the phone tightly, his news suddenly meaningless. His father kept talking, his voice brimming with anticipation. "Soon enough, only the working class will bear the tax burden. The deficits won't matter; the real money will funnel to us. We're winning, Anthony, and you've got a place in this if you know how to keep up."

Anthony swallowed hard, struggling to keep his voice steady. "Sure, Dad. It sounds... big. I just wanted to share my news too."

Barton gave a faint, distracted chuckle. "Oh, yes. Good for you, Director, right? Sure, sure. Keep working hard. But remember, we're talking about something bigger than your job." His voice softened, almost reverent. "We're about to become the voice they trust. The only voice."

And with that, the line went dead. Anthony stared at the phone, the weight of his father's indifference settling over him, familiar as an old ache. Once again, Barton's world had no space for his son's interests.

Chapter 16: The Caseloads Quagmire

Anthony sat staring at a confusing spreadsheet on his computer screen. All the colors and numbers created an unintelligible data collage; it may as well have been written in a foreign language. His new role as Specialized Student Care Director had come with a heftier paycheck, more authority, and a general sense of accomplishment. But now, for the first time, he was facing a problem that he couldn't just finesse his way out of. The Occupational Therapists, OTs for short, were in disarray, and Anthony, with his questionable qualifications and aversion to high expectations, had no idea how to solve it.

The issue had started as a murmur—a few OTs grumbling about uneven caseloads, or something like that. But the murmurs grew louder, spreading like wildfire through the group. Anthony quickly realized this was a bigger problem than he'd anticipated.

Some of the OTs, scattered across 80 schools in six districts, were drowning in referrals and long commutes, while others were coasting with fewer students and shorter drives. Their travel times were all over the map. Some were driving two hours between schools, while others made it from one to the next in under five minutes. There were ten OTs in total, not all full-time, but most were adamant their workload was unfair compared to the others. And as Anthony soon discovered, managing this group was like herding cats.

He called a meeting to address the issue, hoping to get a handle on the situation. What followed was nothing short of chaos.

The meeting room was a mess of overlapping conversations before it even began. Anthony stood at the front of the room, watching in silence as the OTs settled in, though "settled" was a generous term. There was Sheila, the loud and boisterous OT, who never hesitated to speak her mind, and almost always at full volume.

She was already complaining about the commute to her distant schools, waving her arms for emphasis. In contrast, there was Mary, quiet and reserved, who barely said a word unless directly asked. Her workload was manageable, and she was fine with things staying as they were. In fact, she seemed more interested in avoiding any change at all. Then there was Gene, who might have been just a little off his rocker. He had a habit of steering every conversation toward conspiracy theories about how the administration was "out to get the therapists" and micromanage them into submission.

As the rest of the OTs shuffled into the room, it became clear that no one agreed on anything, and Anthony could already feel the enormity of the tension.

Anthony took a deep breath and called the meeting to order, trying to sound authoritative. "All right, let's get started."

Sheila immediately raised her hand and, without waiting to be called on, launched into her complaint. "I'm covering five schools, all with high numbers, across two counties! I'm in the car more than I'm in the schools! Meanwhile, half the people in this room are sitting pretty with half the work I have." Mary, with her arms crossed, glanced around the room but said nothing; she had no intention of increasing her workload. Gene, meanwhile, was already scribbling furiously in his notebook, muttering something about bureau incompetence and manipulation.

Anthony opened his laptop, prepared to unveil his solution. He wasn't sure how well it would go over, mainly because he didn't understand the solution himself. He had a spreadsheet, or what he thought was a spreadsheet, that was designed to help evenly distribute the caseloads and travel times. The problem was, the numbers didn't really add up. He had thrown in random figures here and there, subtracted numbers when things looked off, and hoped that no one would notice that none of it made sense.

He projected the spreadsheet onto the screen. The numbers were there, neatly arranged. He had columns for caseloads, columns for drive times, and even a mysterious column labeled "Effort

Multiplier," a figure Anthony had completely invented. He even added in a "correction factor" for no other reason than to make the totals look more even.

"All right," Anthony began, trying to sound confident, "this is a breakdown of everyone's caseload and drive times. As you can see, I've factored effort and travel, to try to balance things out more fairly."

Sheila leaned forward, squinting at the screen. "What's the 'Effort Multiplier' supposed to mean?"

Anthony coughed. "That's... that's a calculation I put together to account for the time you spend preparing for each student versus the time you're driving."

"And how did you come up with that number?" Sheila shot back.

"I... well, it's based on a range of factors," Anthony replied vaguely. He could feel the sweat starting to form on the back of his neck.

Gene snorted from the back of the room. "Looks like a load of crap to me. What are you trying to pull here?"

Anthony cleared his throat, realizing this wasn't going well. The room was beginning to stir with discontent. Mary, ever the silent observer, raised her hand, surprising everyone.

"I think," she said quietly, "that we should just leave things the way they are. This is making everything more complicated than it needs to be."

Sheila rolled her eyes. "Of course you'd say that. You've got the easiest caseload here!"

Anthony felt his control slipping. The room was devolving into arguments, and his half-baked spreadsheet wasn't helping. In fact, it was making things worse. The meeting dragged on for another hour, with no resolution in sight. By the end of it, everyone was more frustrated than they were before walking in.

Weeks passed, and the caseload controversy never went away. Anthony had hoped that his spreadsheet, flawed as it was, would at least pacify the group, but it didn't. The OTs continued to grumble about unfair workloads, and while some of them begrudgingly accepted the status quo, others were left seething with resentment.

The school year rolled on, and the therapists turned their attention to managing their cases instead of fighting for change, but the animosity lingered. Burnout was creeping in, especially for those with the heavier workloads, and the tension between the OTs never truly dissipated.

For Anthony, it was a wake-up call. He had bluffed his way through his career, and he had finessed his way into the director's position. But now, faced with a problem that required real leadership, he realized he was in over his head. His Harvard stories, his trivia success, and his easy doctorate hadn't prepared him for the complexities of managing people and workloads.

The OTs, with their eccentric personalities and competing interests, had left him flummoxed. He'd hoped for a quick solution, but instead, he found himself navigating a world of chaos. As the controversy simmered in the background, Anthony couldn't shake the feeling that it was only a matter of time before another problem landed on his desk that he wouldn't be able to spreadsheet his way out of.

Chapter 17: Climbing the Ladder

Anthony sat at his desk, staring at a stack of reports he could barely understand. As Director of Specialized Student Care, he knew he was supposed to have a handle on these things, but day by day, it was becoming painfully clear that he didn't. The Occupational Therapist fiasco had proven that much. Despite his best attempts to mediate their caseload dispute, he'd been unable to bring any real solution to the table. His weak attempts to appease both sides had only served to deepen their frustration, and eventually, things had returned to the status quo, with the therapists more resentful than ever and no changes in sight.

It wasn't his first failure as director, nor would it be the last. Another near miss came when he overlooked a critical budget allocation for adaptive equipment. The oversight left several students without the tools they needed to participate in class, and it wasn't until a school counselor flagged it that he even realized the mistake. Frantically, he reallocated funds from another budget line, framing it as "revised resource prioritization." To his relief, the Commissioner accepted his explanation without much scrutiny. But the experience rattled him; he couldn't keep relying on quick fixes to sidestep responsibility forever.

He needed an escape route. That's when it hit him: why not aim for the Commissioner role? Tanner Smith, the current Commissioner, was nearing retirement. And who better to take over than the Director of Specialized Student Care? Special education was, after all, the heart of the bureau's services to its districts, and he'd been in the department long enough to know the basics. Plus, he held a doctorate in education—credentials that would certainly play well with the board.

Anthony's dream began to crystallize. As Commissioner, he could hire skilled people to handle the day-to-day work, allowing him to insulate himself from the operational mess he was never able to manage. All he'd need to do was maintain relationships with the board, show up for big moments, and accept praise for others' accomplishments. It was a perfect vision.

But the calendar couldn't move fast enough. Tanner didn't seem in any rush to leave, and as months passed, Anthony found himself watching for any sign that Tanner's retirement might be near. Each failure in his own department made his impatience grow. He found himself cultivating connections, positioning himself strategically with board members by attending every meeting and contributing comments that hinted at his "long-term vision." He was careful to mention his education, subtly bringing up his Harvard degree whenever he could, ensuring the board remembered his academic pedigree.

In the meantime, he continued to sidestep conflicts in his department, choosing his words carefully to avoid making any real decisions. When a compliance audit revealed significant delays in assessments, he framed it as an issue with outdated tracking systems rather than a shortfall in his leadership. He swiftly organized a task force to "update assessment protocols," placating the board with the promise of change and buying himself more time. But each near miss only reinforced his resolve: he needed to rise higher, to a role where he could maintain control from a safe distance.

He even hinted at his ambition to Tanner. Over drinks, he leaned in, feigning humility as he said, "You know, Tanner, I've always felt that my career's leading me toward bigger challenges. The Commissioner role—that's where I feel I could really make a difference." Tanner, who seemed halfway out the door already, had merely nodded and sipped his drink.

Each passing month, Tanner's retirement seemed more certain, but Anthony knew he couldn't leave anything to chance. He developed a war chest of talking points, stockpiling every small accomplishment he could twist into a qualification. He quietly gathered favors, solidifying his reputation in the bureau as a steady, reliable figure. And then, finally, the day came. Tanner announced his retirement, and Anthony moved quickly, positioning himself as the ideal candidate to the board. He emphasized his years of service, his steady hand, and his "intimate understanding" of the bureau's needs.

But he wasn't the only candidate. Leon Miller, the Assistant Superintendent from the largest school district within the bureau's region, had thrown his hat in the ring. Leon was older and nearing retirement himself, but he had a strong reputation, with a record of proven programs and years of successful leadership. Anthony hoped the board would prefer a younger, long-term candidate like himself, someone who'd be around to see things through. Surely his loyalty, his education, and his long-standing connections would give him the edge.

The interview day finally arrived. Anthony entered with polished confidence, ready to deploy his carefully honed talking points. He emphasized his tenure, his dedication, his experience in navigating the complexities of special education. Everything seemed to be going smoothly—until the board asked a question he hadn't prepared for: "What initiatives have you accomplished as an administrator?"

The question struck like a hammer. Anthony's mind raced, grasping for any example of leadership or innovation. But the truth was glaring; he had no notable achievements to point to. His tenure as director had been a series of near misses and close calls, none of which he could present as accomplishments. He managed a weak response about "supporting existing frameworks," but it was clear his answer lacked substance.

A week later, the decision came in. Anthony hadn't been chosen. Tanner Smith's replacement would be Leon Miller. It was a no brainer. He had years of proven leadership, solid initiatives, and a calming steady hand. The board had opted for his experience over Anthony's tenure, but there was a twist.

The board directed Leon to offer Anthony the role of Assistant Commissioner. Their rationale was clear: Anthony was a valuable asset to the bureau, and they wanted him to continue growing as a leader, preparing for the eventual top role once Leon retired. Anthony couldn't deny that it was a smart move, but it wasn't what he had hoped for.

When Leon Miller called Anthony into his office to discuss the offer, the conversation was awkward from the start. Leon wasn't exactly thrilled to have a middleman, but he respected Anthony and wanted to set the right tone for their working relationship.

"Well, Anthony," Leon began, adjusting his glasses, "the board thinks it'd be good for you to step into the role of Assistant Commissioner. They see your potential and want you to gain more leadership experience under my guidance."

Anthony smiled, though he felt a bit stung. He had hoped to take Tanner's seat, not the one just below it. But still, this was a significant promotion, and the pay increase was tempting, and most importantly, he'd be insulated from managing the specialists. "I appreciate that, Leon. I do, but 'Assistant Commissioner'... well, I was thinking more along the lines of Deputy Commissioner."

Leon raised an eyebrow. "Deputy? It's the same role. What's in a name?"

"True," Anthony replied smoothly, "but 'Deputy' carries a bit more weight. It reflects the level of responsibility I'm ready to take on, and, of course, there's a slight difference in pay. Oh, and one more thing, I'm not taking any shit."

Leon looked at Anthony for a long moment, as though weighing the ridiculousness of the negotiation. "I'll talk to the board. I'm sure it'll be fine." Just like that, Anthony secured the title of Deputy Commissioner.

As Deputy Commissioner, Anthony quickly realized the role suited him far better than being Director of Specialized Student Care ever had. His primary responsibility was to listen to the concerns of department directors and offer "guidance," which usually boiled down to encouraging relationship building and navigating challenges diplomatically. He rarely had to offer real solutions. In fact, whenever he was asked for input on a particularly thorny issue, his go-to response became, "It's important to build strong relationships. That's how we get things done here."

When school district leaders expressed concerns about staffing shortages or budget constraints, Anthony would nod sympathetically and suggested that perhaps more funding for new initiatives was the answer. It wasn't a real solution, but it was enough to keep conversations going without addressing the problem.

In truth, he had no desire to overhaul the system or implement any ambitious new programs. His goal was to maintain the status quo, keep people happy, and stay insulated from the day-to-day operational headaches that had plagued him as a department head.

As far as Anthony was concerned, life was good. He now had more authority, a better salary, and significantly less pressure. The board had effectively groomed him to take over one day, and the only person he had to answer to was Leon, whose job it was to prepare Anthony for his eventual promotion. It was a win-win.

Sitting in his office, feet up on his desk, Anthony couldn't help but feel proud. Being Deputy Commissioner had turned out to be a perfect fit. He found a way to rise through the ranks without any heavy lifting, and for the first time in his career, he felt completely comfortable. All he must do now is to wait for Leon Miller to retire, and then, finally, the top job will be his.

Chapter 18: Ashes and Aftermath

Anthony sat alone in his office while the usual drone of his workday muted to an uncomfortable hum. His eyes lingered on the worn cardboard box on his desk, stamped with the Hampden County seal—a box as unremarkable as the people it contained. Inside lay the final remnants of Barton and Sue Pollock, reduced to two small urns. The dull gray metal of each urn, simple and identical, felt like an insult. There was no warmth, no final message, no trace of the parents he'd reached out to all those years. Just this: dust and debt.

When the county clerk's letter had arrived, clipped and perfunctory—We regret to inform you of the deaths of Barton and Sue Pollock—he felt nothing at first. Then a hollow ache began to swell, a mix of anger, confusion, and the faintest twinge of grief. He'd spent his life trying to be something for them, something they might acknowledge, respect, or even love. He'd called them when he was nearing graduation, when he got engaged, even when he landed this position as Director, but they'd always treated him like a stranger passing through.

He tore the tape, peeling back the cardboard lid with a grimace, the stale smell of paper and metal wafting up. The two urns sat wedged in the box, each cold and lifeless, side by side like strangers forced together in a waiting room. Beneath them lay stacks of receipts, foreclosure notices, medical bills, debts they had scraped together like loose change, leaving him a final legacy of borrowed dimes and unpaid balances.

A bitter laugh escaped him, sharp and low. All these years, he'd clung to the hope that his father might recognize his efforts, maybe even feel a flicker of pride in his son's success. He'd imagined Barton, if only for a second, picking up the phone with something close to approval in his voice. But Barton left him the same way he lived with him—cold, indifferent, caught up in his own twisted ambitions.

He ran his thumb along the rim of one urn, the rough metal cool against his skin. This, then, was the end of it. He wasn't the heir to anything except the hollow ideals Barton had preached. Barton had spent his life playing the puppeteer, pulling strings and whispering his own brand of power, but he left nothing that mattered. Just gray dust and debt.

A soft knock on his office door broke his thoughts, followed by a hesitant voice. "Anthony?" It was Debby, his assistant. Her voice, usually brisk, held an unexpected gentleness.

He looked up, his expression hardening instinctively. "What is it Debby?"

She entered, looking slightly hesitant but composed. "Mr. Pollock," she said, "Leon Miller wants to see you. He mentioned it was about his retirement announcement."

Anthony blinked, a jolt of realization electrifying him. The news he'd been waiting for—years of preparing, navigating, enduring—was finally here. For a split second, he forgot the urns entirely. Optimism surged through him, drowning out the gloom he'd been carrying since receiving his parents' remains. Without a second thought, he hastily shoved the urns into a drawer, closing it firmly. Let them gather dust, he thought coldly.

In that instant, he recognized how much his parents' welfare truly mattered to him—just as little as his had mattered to them. He felt a detached sort of satisfaction, as if he were finally aligning with the legacy his father had meant to leave behind, one that valued control over connection.

Straightening his tie, he left his office, a sense of liberation spreading through him. The past had no hold here; this moment was his, the culmination of his calculated ambition. He wasn't going to waste another minute mourning people who would never mourn for him. Barton taught him, in his own twisted way, to keep moving forward, to pursue power unflinchingly. And now, he'd do just that.

As he strode down the hallway toward Leon's office, a sense of excitement welled up within him. He would embrace this moment and live it fully, no longer shackled by memories of his parents. This was the next step, his long-awaited victory on the horizon.

Inside Leon's office, Anthony took his seat, barely able to contain the anticipation. Today, his years of patience and careful maneuvering were about to pay off. The top position, the very life he'd spent so long waiting to inherit, lay within reach.

Chapter 19: The Allure of Power

Anthony leaned back in his leather chair with his gaze fixed on the brass nameplate that now gleamed on his office door: Commissioner. Years of strategic maneuvering, waiting for the right people to step aside, had brought him here. His heart raced at the thought of the title he had finally claimed. Yet as he sat alone, thoughts of his father's legacy crept back, hollowing out what should have felt like victory.

He closed his eyes, in an attempt to force out the image of Barton Pollock—the father who had never cared, even at the end, who only left Anthony a legacy of debts and disappointment. Barton had spent his life pulling strings, bending people to his will, yet he'd died without a trace of acknowledgment for his only son. Anthony's hands curled into fists as he leaned forward, forcing himself to refocus. His father was gone. Anthony's new title, this unchecked power, was his. It had come at the expense of those he'd outmaneuvered, and Anthony could almost hear Barton's voice telling him, for the first time: Well done!

But his authority now required action. Little Horizons Child Care, a persistent thorn, had been hounding the bureau for services they didn't qualify for. The requests had always come from various administrators, but this time it was different; the name on the request was Delilah Annette, a new assistant. Intrigued, Anthony decided to handle it personally, imagining how satisfying it would be to put an end to their appeals once and for all.

Walking up to Little Horizons, he admired his reflection in the glass entry doors, feeling the cloak of authority settle around him. He built his influence piece by piece, and now he could wield it however he saw fit. As he approached the front desk, he was unprepared for the sight that awaited him.

Delilah, a tall, fit, beautiful blonde bombshell was standing behind the front desk, with bright eyes and a welcoming expression. Her long hair framed her face perfectly, reminiscent of the girls who had captivated him in his youth. She moved with a fluid grace that seemed effortless, and when she looked up, her gaze met him directly, unwavering and warm. The contrast to the usual formality he encountered took him off guard, leaving him feeling, just for a moment, exposed.

"Mr. Pollock," she greeted him, extending her hand, her voice carrying a slight lilt that drew him in. "Thank you for coming. I'm so pleased we could meet in person."

Anthony nodded, voice even. "Yes, of course. I'm here to discuss your request," he said, doing his best to sound in control.

They moved to a small meeting room, and Delilah began her presentation with an ease and charm that surprised him. Her argument for Little Horizons' case was meticulous, compelling, and her words carried a conviction he found unexpectedly captivating. But it wasn't the argument that caught his attention. Her perfume lingered in the air, subtly sweet, and her eyes, animated and intent, never wavered from his as she spoke. Every gesture, every slight lean in his direction, felt inviting and intoxicating.

Anthony realized, as the meeting continued, that she wasn't just persuasive; she was effortlessly commanding his attention. He was reminded of the girls he had admired from afar in school, those who had never spared him a second glance. But here was Delilah, a woman whose interest seemed genuine, who seemed to see him as someone worthy of her time. His usual reserve slipped, replaced by an impulse he could hardly explain nor defend.

"Delilah," he interrupted, his voice carrying a new boldness, "I have an offer for you."

She paused with evident curiosity. "An offer?" she repeated, with a spark in her eyes.

"Yes," he said, leaning forward, as an idea was taking shape. "I want you to come work for me at Mountain View. I'm creating a new position—Director of Ingenuity—and I think you'd be perfect for it."

The words left his mouth before he'd completely thought them through, but he didn't pull back. He saw her as a potential ally, someone who could not only support his goals but also add a touch of sophistication to his team. He could sense that she was calculating, intelligent, and adaptable, qualities that would serve him well.

Delilah raised an eyebrow, clearly intrigued. "Director of Ingenuity? I can't say I've heard of that position before," she replied, a slight smile playing at her lips.

He felt a thrill at her interest. "It's a new role," he replied ad hoc. "You have the qualities I need—vision, creativity, and the ability to handle people." He held her gaze. "I'm looking for someone who can bring fresh ideas to the bureau."

Her eyes softened, and he saw a flicker of something— recognition, perhaps, or a shared understanding of ambition. "It's an intriguing proposition," she said thoughtfully. "I'll need a little time to consider it."

Anthony nodded, handing her his business card, his hand brushing hers. A charge ran through him, a thrill he hadn't felt in years. "Take all the time you need," he said, his voice quieter.

When he left Little Horizons, his mind raced with possibilities. Delilah Annette wasn't just an assistant at some rink-a-dink day care anymore; she was a potential ally, someone who could help him build the influence he envisioned. With her by his side, he felt the stirrings of a future he could shape, a world where he could wield real power.

Later that evening, Delilah drove home, her thoughts on the meeting. She understood the opportunity of Anthony's offer and knew what lay beneath it. Director of Ingenuity—an invented role, born from his desire to keep her close, to draw her into his orbit. It was clear to her that Anthony Pollock saw something in her he wanted to cultivate, maybe even control.

When she walked through the front door, her husband, Carl, looked up with mild curiosity. She slipped off her coat, letting the weight of the day settle around her.

"I was offered a new position today," she said, settling into a chair across from him.

Carl raised an eyebrow. "A new position?"

"At the Mountain View Regional Education Bureau," she replied, savoring the words. "Director of Ingenuity."

He looked puzzled. "What does that mean?"

She smirked, leaning back. "It means I know exactly what he wants and how to use it." She met her husband's gaze. "He's into me. I'll play the part, Carl. There's no risk. I just have to charm him and offer obedience. This could triple my salary."

Carl's enthusiasm was a bit reserved, "I like the idea of a salary bump, but I don't like the idea of your boss fawning all over you."

"He's not anywhere in your league Carl. He's old, short, and a dork. I'm just not going to let him know my true feelings." Delilah replied with a light air of superiority. "He was wearing a wedding ring. If things ever take a turn, I'll just bring up our marriages as an escape."

Carl chuckled, shaking his head in admiration. "Then it sounds like you've got it all under control. Does this mean we can start having kids? You'll be bringing in enough money to make it work."

"In your dreams," Delilah clapped back. "I don't want my body all bent out of shape. Besides, I've been working with kids long enough to know that I don't want to bring one home with me."

"My mom," Delilah sat up to dig her cell phone out of her purse. "She's going to be beside herself. I need to fill her in."

"Tell Lilith I said hi." Carl injected, encouraging the call. "She will be so proud of you. All her struggles are finally paying off. Have her come over for dinner. We'll get takeout."

That night the three of them huddled over pizza, recalling all their previous struggles and feeling they can laugh about them now. It was all in the past, and the future looked bright.

Chapter 20: The Meeting Mobs

Anthony, mindful of maintaining connections with the districts he serves, reluctantly accepted Superintendent Linda Mason's invitation to their board meeting. Her district had become a battleground. They were plagued by activists who had transformed these meetings into chaotic spectacles. Linda wanted more than an ally; she needed a fresh perspective—someone who could help her navigate the storm and restore focus to the essential work of education.

The school board meeting room at Sunrise Hills High School wasn't built for spectacle. Rows of metal folding chairs sat beneath harsh fluorescent lights, with walls adorned with cheerful messages declaring "Education is for Everyone." Tonight, those words felt hollow, swallowed by the electric tension in the air. Anthony adjusted his tie and glanced at Linda, who stood behind the podium, gripping the sides like it was her shield.

"This is what we've been enduring for months," she whispered with wearied exhaustion. "Brace yourself."

Anthony nodded, but he wasn't ready. He wasn't prepared for the sea of angry faces packed into the room, for the signs scrawled in thick marker—Protect Our Kids! Stop the Indoctrination!—or for the palpable hostility that rolled off the crowd like a physical force. He wasn't ready for the venom in their voices, the fervor in their eyes.

The meeting began uneventfully enough. Linda called it to order with a calm but strained voice. The board members were seated at a long table facing the crowd. They sifted through their papers and avoided eye contact with the audience. As soon as the first agenda item was introduced, the room's tension erupted like a volcano under pressure.

A man wearing a trucker hat emblazoned with an American flag made of bullets and a T-shirt that read *Don't Tread on Me* shouted with a booming voice, "Why are you teaching our kids to hate America?"

Linda raised her hands in a placating gesture. "Sir, we're not... "

"Don't lie to us!" the man bellowed, cutting her off. "I've seen the materials. You're teaching them that America is racist. That our founding fathers were criminals. You're turning them against their own country!"

Linda took a deep breath, her grip on the podium tightening. "I assure you, our curriculum hasn't changed in decades. We're using the same state-approved text that you learned from as a child. They cover history comprehensively, including difficult topics, but... "

"Comprehensively? You mean brainwashing!" someone shouted from the back.

A woman wearing a shirt that read *Baby Momma* stepped forward, her face flushed with anger. "You're trying to make our kids feel ashamed for being white. That's not education, that's propaganda!"

Anthony sat frozen, his stomach churning. Linda's words were logical and measured, but they ricocheted off the crowd like pebbles against steel. They weren't seeking logic or the truth. They wanted an ounce of flesh for crimes never committed.

"Let's all remain civil," Linda said, though her voice trembled slightly. "We're here to address your concerns, but we need to do so respectfully."

Respect, Anthony thought bitterly, had no place here. This wasn't a conversation. It was a battlefield.

The night continued to spiral. One after another, speakers approached the microphone, each more outraged than the last. They railed against critical race theory, though none seemed to understand what it was—let alone that it's only taught in college courses. They warned of grooming and accused the district of "sexualizing" children, citing vague anecdotes and YouTube clips as evidence. They demanded book bans for titles they hadn't read but had heard were dangerous.

One man slammed a book down on the podium with theatrical force. "This filth is in our library!" he shouted, flipping through the pages. "This is pornography, plain and simple. And you're giving it to our kids!"

Linda leaned into her microphone, her voice calm but firm. "Sir, that book is a Pulitzer Prize-winning novel. It's part of the high school's AP English curriculum, approved by the state."

"It doesn't matter what prize it won!" the man shot back. "It's corrupting their minds!"

Anthony scanned the room, his eyes settling on the faces in the crowd. They were parents, grandparents, and neighbors, ordinary people who should have been allies of the school, not its enemies. But their expressions were twisted with anger, their voices shrill with fear. He recognized the signs: they were puppets, their strings pulled by unseen hands.

His stomach turned as he thought of his father who made an art of planting these types of seeds. Barton's carefully curated conspiracy theories started small, just whispers on late-night radio and fringe forums. But they had grown, spreading like weeds, choking out reason and trust. And now, here they were, adults screaming about imaginary dangers, their paranoia nurtured by opportunists who thrived on chaos.

Linda pressed on, attempting to answer questions that had no logical basis. "No, we're not replacing history with Marxism," she said, her tone fraying. "Yes, we support the rights of all students to feel safe and included, but we're not 'pushing an agenda.' These are legal requirements, not personal choices."

But the crowd wasn't interested in legalities. When one accusation was dismantled, they latched onto another. When their claims were disproved, they doubled down, insisting the evidence itself was a lie.

A woman in a floral dress took the microphone, her voice trembling with righteous fury. "You say you care about all students, but what about our kids? The normal ones. Why are you catering to the fringe, to the... the confused? What about the majority?"

Anthony grasped her despair as Linda responded, her voice buckling under the strain. "We don't prioritize one group of students over another. Every child deserves a safe and supportive environment."

"But you're not supporting us!" the woman shrieked. "You're tearing apart the moral fabric of this community!"

A cheer erupted from the crowd, the applause loud enough to rattle the windows. Anthony glanced at Linda, whose face was pale, her hands trembling as she held the edges of the podium. The board members exchanged nervous glances; their earlier composure now replaced with barely masked panic.

By the time the meeting adjourned, Anthony felt like he had endured something between a witch trial and an angry mob lynching party. He stood near the back of the room, watching as Linda fielded one last barrage of questions from angry parents. She looked hollowed-out, a mere shell of the confident administrator she had been hours earlier.

"Well," she said, turning to Anthony as the crowd retired for the night. "What did you think?"

Anthony shook his head, searching for the right words. "I think you're fighting a losing battle."

Linda's laugh was dry, bitter. "You're not kidding."

Driving home that night, Anthony replayed the meeting in his mind. The chaos, the anger, the sheer irrationality of it all, it was horrifying, yes, but it also felt... familiar. This wasn't new. This was his father's legacy, rebranded for a new generation. Barton had built his influence on paranoia and division, and the fruit of that labor was now ripening across the nation.

Anthony clinched his steering wheel with white knuckles. He didn't want to be part of this fight. Let them scream, he thought. Let them destroy themselves. It wasn't his problem.

And yet, as he pulled into his driveway, the echoes of the meeting clung to him, refusing to fade. No matter how much he tried to convince himself otherwise, Anthony couldn't escape the truth: the fire his father had ignited wasn't dying, it was spreading. The thought of it reaching his bureau sent a chill through him. He resolved to avoid invitations to neighboring school board meetings in the future, preferring to keep a low profile and sidestep the chaos. He would frame it as a strategic choice; focusing on long-term planning rather than entangling himself in volatile local disputes. The reality, though, was simpler: he didn't care enough to confront the mobs. It was easier to turn away, letting others deal with the fallout.

Chapter 21: Fumbling and Flattery

From the moment Delilah assumed her role as Director of Ingenuity, she understood that her job had little to do with strategy or vision. She knew her real task lay in keeping Anthony Pollock entranced. She'd nurture the thinly veiled desire he harbored under layers of pride and ambition. She didn't kid herself about her lack of qualifications; her office wasn't earned, it was gifted, because Anthony craved what she brought: a tantalizing mixture of adoration and allure.

Anthony hadn't appointed her for her skills, and Delilah saw no point in pretending otherwise. Instead, she wielded her real talents with precision. She made him feel brilliant, necessary, as if the bureau's success hinged entirely on his genius. She painted him as the visionary leader he longed to be. Anthony soaked it up, that hunger in him insatiable. She could see it in the way he looked at her, that glint of admiration mingled with something darker.

But the honeymoon phase between them had limits, and those boundaries were tested the moment Delilah faced the actual responsibilities of her role. Leading a department of seasoned professionals felt like attempting to steer a ship she'd only ever seen from the shore. Team meetings descended into painful exercises as she floundered, reaching for experience she didn't possess. She stumbled through corporate phrases she didn't understand, spouting jargon she hoped sounded impressive but didn't fool anyone.

In one meeting, she stood at the head of the conference table, nodding as if her vague words held weight. "We need to focus on maximizing our ingenuity pipeline," she declared, her voice confident but empty. "Let's align our actionable takeaways with optimized synergies."

Her team exchanged glances that bordered on exasperation. Nicole, a seasoned employee with little patience for buzzwords, finally spoke up with carefully measured restraint. "Delilah, what exactly is an *'ingenuity pipeline'*? And... how do we optimize it?"

Delilah's eyes flickered, betraying her discomfort. She searched for words, her gaze darting around the room for an unspoken lifeline. "That's a good question, Nicole," she managed, masking her nerves with a brittle smile. "But let's keep our focus on the big picture for now."

The response landed like a lead balloon. Her team watched her in a silence thick with judgment, their expressions betraying a shared frustration. When the meeting finally ended, Delilah swept out of the room, her composure barely intact, and went straight to Anthony.

"Anthony," she murmured, her voice laced with vulnerability, "I think there's tension in the team. They're not giving me a fair chance."

Anthony's face darkened, his protectiveness flaring. "They're not team players," he dismissed with a wave. "They'll come around, Delilah. You deserve subordinates that respect your leadership."

Delilah's lips curved into a grateful smile, her hand brushing his arm just long enough to convey the unspoken intimacy between them. She made him feel like her knight, her defender, the one person she could rely on to shield her from the scrutiny of others. She played the role perfectly, and Anthony fell for it, the admiration in her gaze was a drug he couldn't resist.

But that devotion carried a price, a line he danced along every day with growing recklessness. Delilah's attention filled a void in him, her praise giving life to the image he had long cultivated. She made him feel like he was destined for something greater than he'd ever dreamed. Yet each time he basked in her veneration, a sliver of guilt gnawed at him, tugging him back to the face of his wife, Cynthia, who waited for him at home, blissfully unaware of the tangled emotions roiling within him.

He told himself he wasn't betraying Cynthia, that his connection with Delilah was harmless, nothing more than professional reverence. But each glance, each lingering touch, said otherwise. At times, he found himself justifying it, telling himself that Delilah's homage was a necessary indulgence, a small gift he allowed himself in exchange for loyalty. But deep down, he felt the deception, the shadow of Cynthia's love hanging over him, tightening with each lie he told himself.

In one all-staff meeting, Delilah took her flattery public, a bold move that caught everyone off guard. She rose from her seat, turning to face him, her eyes brimming with feigned reverence. "I just want to take a moment to thank Anthony," she began, her voice filled with practiced awe. "Your vision and leadership have transformed this organization. You're an inspiration to all of us."

Anthony felt his face flush, his chest swelling as her words washed over him. For a brief, shining moment, he felt invincible, every past insecurity erased under the spotlight of her praise. He glanced around the room, meeting the eyes of his colleagues, basking in the awe he imagined reflected in their gazes.

But across the table, Alice, the Director of Information, watched the performance with thinly veiled contempt. She'd tolerated Delilah's incompetence, her meaningless jargon, her endless appeal to Anthony for protection, but this was too much. Alice cleared her throat, unwilling to let Delilah's sycophancy outshine her.

"I second that," she said, her tone strained as she met Anthony's gaze. "Your leadership... has certainly been impactful." The words fell a little short, and Anthony detected the faintest edge of sarcasm in her tone. But he brushed it off, too absorbed in the rush of idolatry to care about the skepticism simmering around him.

As the meeting wrapped up, he caught Delilah's eye across the room. She offered him a private smile, a look meant only for him, and he felt a surge of satisfaction that clouded every doubt. They shared an unspoken understanding, a bond that went beyond words, and for that brief moment, the approval of his team, his loyalty to Cynthia—

none of it mattered. Delilah saw him for the visionary he believed himself to be, and that was her role.

But whispers began to spread, the murmurs grew louder as his colleagues exchanged glances behind closed doors. Anthony could feel the discontent, the way his team resented Delilah's incompetence, her reliance on empty phrases and constant appeal for his protection. He ignored the signs, telling himself that their loyalty didn't matter, that if Delilah held him in high regard, he could weather the criticism.

At home, Cynthia waited, her steady love was an anchor he relied on more than he realized. She didn't question his late nights or the distant look in his eyes; she trusted him without reservation, a loyalty he felt he hadn't earned. The guilt of his emotional affair with Delilah weighed heavily, each moment of flattery another nail in the coffin of his fidelity. Cynthia deserved more than the fractured devotion he offered, but each time he felt that pang of regret, Delilah's gaze pulled him back, her admiration a balm to his fragile ego.

As the days passed, he found himself slipping deeper into the role Delilah had crafted for him, his attraction to her a constant whisper in the back of his mind. He convinced himself he could have both worlds, that he could honor Cynthia while indulging in Delilah's worship. But he knew, somewhere in the shadows of his mind, that the line he walked grew thinner every day.

For now, Delilah was his muse, his inspiration, the spark that fueled his ambition. He'd protect her, ignore the murmurs of his colleagues, and cling to the illusion that he could balance both worlds.

He didn't know where it would end, but he was too far down the rabbit hole to turn back now.

Delilah Annette had mastered survival in her role as Director of Ingenuity, a position that was vague by design. She didn't bother learning the job's nuances or grasping its demands. Her role was about enchantment. She knew exactly how to keep Anthony enthralled, which was her specialty. So, when her latest "initiative" to streamline the Specialized Student Care Department nearly imploded, she barely flinched. The only person who could really make trouble was Margaret Sanders, and Margaret wasn't her problem. Not anymore.

It started innocently enough. Delilah had wandered into the world of special education like a trespasser in a foreign land, brimming with buzzwords and clueless ambition. She threw around phrases like "optimizing resource allocation" and "simplifying service workflows" without the faintest grasp of the legal boundaries binding every decision. And she might have continued unchecked if Margaret hadn't stepped in.

Margaret, who became Director of Specialized Student Care after Anthony's promotion, stormed into Delilah's office one afternoon, her eyes blazing with indignation. "Delilah, what exactly do you think you're doing?" she demanded, her voice slicing through Delilah's equilibrium. "Special education is a legal minefield, not a pet project for you to 'optimize.' You're making changes without any idea of the repercussions. If you don't stop, you're going to drag the entire bureau into legal jeopardy."

Delilah put on her brightest smile. "Oh, Margaret, I was only trying to help. Make things more efficient."

"Efficient?" Margaret's face was a mask of controlled fury. "Do you even understand what that word means in this context? Special education isn't something you can just 'tweak' on a whim. This stops now, Delilah."

Margaret left, her back straight, her purpose clear. For a moment, Delilah sat at her desk, stunned, the enormity of her blunder settled over her. But she wasn't about to let Margaret ruin her carefully woven facade. Within minutes, she gathered herself and walked to Anthony's office, every step a calculated act of desperation.

She knocked lightly, then entered without waiting for a response. "Anthony," she whispered, her voice a mix of distress and vulnerability, "do you have a moment?"

Anthony glanced up, caught off guard. Seeing her there, looking so distraught, sent a rush through him. He motioned for her to sit, his eyes locked on hers as she leaned forward, offering the faintest glimpse down her blouse. The sight held him captive, his focus narrowing to the moment. When he finally looked up, the scent of her perfume and the quiet need in her eyes was intoxicating.

"It's Margaret," she began, her voice low and filled with carefully crafted uncertainty. "She's... obstructing me. I try to make improvements, and she dismisses them. She doesn't respect my position or the vision we're working toward. I don't think she's a team player, Anthony."

He looked at her, surprised. Margaret had been with the bureau forever, a stalwart presence in special education. "Are you sure, Delilah? Margaret's... dedicated. I handpicked her for the job."

Delilah nodded, eyes wide, shining with just the right mix of sadness and resolve. "I am sure. She's set in her ways. She wants to keep everything the same, and that's not what this bureau needs. We need people willing to adapt, to support your vision."

The words hit Anthony like a lightning strike. His vision. She was speaking to him as if he were more than just another Commissioner; she made him feel like a figure of power, someone with a purpose greater than the sum of his title.

"Alright," he said, feeling the thrill of authority rising within him. "I'll talk to her."

The next day, Anthony summoned Margaret to his office. The meeting was brief but pointed. He offered her an early retirement, framing it as an opportunity for "fresh leadership." Margaret saw through the pretense, her expression grim but accepting. She negotiated her terms with a quiet resolve, arranging a substantial retirement bonus and agreeing to remain until a replacement could be found.

But Margaret wasn't going to let her department fall into inexperienced hands. Days turned into weeks. But finally, one day, while Margaret was planning her transition, a call came from Joy Denison, a respected Director at a neighboring bureau, curious about Mountain View's compliance success. Margaret seized the opportunity, steering the conversation toward her soon-to-be vacant position, subtly suggesting that Joy might be the ideal candidate.

By the time Joy ended the call, she was intrigued. Relocating to a place where she loves to visit, working within a bureau known for its success with state compliance; it was a chance she couldn't turn down. Margaret had played her part skillfully, and soon Joy was set to take over, a seasoned professional to replace her.

When Anthony heard that Joy would accept the position, relief washed over him. Margaret could transition smoothly, and Joy would handle the intricacies of special education without requiring his oversight. Delilah would be pleased, and he could focus on loftier goals.

Delilah practically floated into his office when she learned the news. She moved to his side, her eyes gleaming with something he could only describe as reverence.

"Anthony, you're amazing!" she whispered, leaning close. Her hand brushed his shoulder, lingering just a moment longer than necessary. "You're not just a Commissioner, you're a big-dick CEO. I swear, if we weren't both married, I'd... let's just say, I'll be thinking about you tonight."

The words struck him like a drug, flooding him with a rush he's never felt. Big-dick CEO. The title reverberated in his mind, each word a powerful note that played to the deepest desires he'd harbored since he was young. This wasn't a promotion or a job title, this was the ultimate validation he'd spent his entire life craving. Someone he admired, someone beautiful, someone who could have any man she wanted, saw him as the power figure he'd always aspired to be. She didn't just respect him; she lusted after him.

"Thank you, Delilah," he managed, trying to contain his exuberance. "That... means a lot."

He knew she was playing him on some level, that her words were carefully chosen, but at that moment, he didn't care. She made him feel invincible, like he could rule the bureau, command loyalty, and bend others to his will. The thrill of being wanted, admired, even lusted after—it all filled him with a kind of intoxicating power. Yet, a strange restraint held him back. Cynthia's face flickered across his mind, a quiet reminder of loyalty, of the life he'd built outside these walls. But Delilah's words blurred those boundaries, and the temptation to act lingered, pulsing beneath the surface.

As Delilah left his office, Anthony leaned back in his chair, basking in the afterglow of her praise. He didn't need to act on her words to feel their impact. Just knowing she saw him that way, that she might desire him as much as he desired her, gave him a new sense of authority.

With Margaret soon gone, Joy stepping in, and Delilah feeding his ego, Anthony felt as though he had finally reached the summit he'd been climbing all his life. He was no longer just the son seeking approval, or the struggling therapist clawing for respect. He had risen. He was the man with the power, the influence, the allure of a "CEO." And as long as Delilah looked at him that way, he knew he'd stay at the top.

The move to Oklahoma was supposed to be the start of something grand. Joy's father painted it as a golden opportunity, a new chapter brimming with possibility. He packed up their modest life in Arkansas with promises of prosperity. They'd chase the hum of oil rigs and the construction boom they fueled. Oklahoma was alive with the smell of fresh asphalt and the din of hammering, a land where fortunes rose as easily as the black gold flowing beneath its soil. For a man in construction, it was the promised land.

Joy clung to his optimism. She loved seeing the excitement in his eyes when he came home each evening, smelling of sawdust and sweat. His boots always leaving a dusty residue across the linoleum floor as he rushed to see his girl. He would lift her into the air and call her his "angel." Her giggles would fill their tiny house like sunshine spilling through a window. They were building something, he'd tell her, not just houses, but a future. A family.

But dreams are fragile things. Oklahoma's promise turned out to be a mirage, shimmering bright but vanishing under the lens of reality. Long hours and financial instability crept into her parents' marriage like a poison, invisible at first, then impossible to ignore. The quiet affection that once saturated their home soured into bickering. The laughter turned into shouting. By the time Joy turned eight, their family was held together by little more than strained smiles at the dinner table. And then, one day, even that was gone.

Her father left, taking his toolbox and his promises with him. They had been abandoned, and the mother who remained was the shadow of the one Joy had known. Bitterness enveloped her and she didn't bother hiding it from Joy. "Your father left us," she'd say, her words laced with venom. "He promised us everything and gave us nothing." It brought Joy great sorrow to have lost everything that once was.

School became her sanctuary. Joy wasn't just a dreamer; she was a fighter. With a mother too busy to guide her and a father who was simply absent, she poured herself into her studies with a determination rooted in resilience. She was determined that her future wouldn't mirror her parents'.

After graduating high school, she became the first in her family to attend college. Enrolling at Oklahoma State, she chose Psychology as her major. The subject fascinated her. She wanted to understand how people thought and why they acted the way they did. She imagined herself helping others make sense of their lives, something she wished someone had done for her.

After graduation, it didn't take long for the reality of her degree to set in. Jobs for psychologists with only a bachelor's were scarce, and the few that existed barely paid a living wage. She felt unfulfilled, as if the promise of her education had been part of an elaborate scheme.

However, Joy didn't give up. She double downed and enrolled in graduate school. This time for a master's degree in School Psychology. The field offered stability, and while it didn't pay as much as clinical psychology, it had something even better: kids. Joy loved children. Their resilience, their potential, she loved their spirit.

It was during graduate school that Joy met David. He wasn't the type to draw attention to himself, but he had a quiet way of making her feel deeply valued. His kindness was steady, his actions thoughtful, never in search of praise. Over time, he became her greatest supporter, taking care of all the loose ends so she could focus on late-night study sessions and her grueling internship.

They married a few years later, right after Joy landed a position at Phantom Lake School District. The timing of her hiring couldn't have been better. It was 2009, and the Great Recession was wreaking havoc across the country. Phantom Lake offered a secure salary in a destabilized world. Joy, who relished the opportunity to help kids, threw herself into her work.

David, however, struggled. The recession gutted his data analytics consulting. He found himself bouncing between jobs that paid far less than he was accustomed to. Joy became the primary breadwinner. Her modest salary was stretched thin as they scraped by. The pressure was relentless, but she held it together, channeling her stress into her work.

A few years later, Joy decided to pursue a doctorate. It wasn't just ambition that drove her, it was an avenue to a better life. She wanted to secure a better future, one where she and David wouldn't have to live paycheck to paycheck. And she sensed that the district was holding back impactful initiatives for reasons that appeared to look like run-of-the-mill apathy. Joy's ambition didn't sit well with her supervisor. Suddenly she was viewed as a threat. She was feared as someone who might outshine him. He began undermining her at every turn, nitpicking her work and questioning her decisions.

Over the course of a few years, her doctorate was nearly complete. Joy knew she had to look elsewhere for advancement. The environment had become toxic, her supervisor's insecurities poisoning her prospects. She began looking for outside opportunities, desperate to escape.

When the offer came from Bleaks Creek Regional Education Bureau, it was both a blessing and a curse. The bureau was small and remote, tucked away in the farthest corner of the state. Its toxic reputation for constant administrative turnover raised red flags. Unfortunately for Joy, she didn't have the luxury of being choosy; her previous employment experience didn't come with a shining recommendation. She accepted the position as Director of Specialized Student Care, determined to make the best of it.

It was immediately clear why administrative turnover was so high. The culture was rancorous, a hornet's nest of resentment and distrust. Longtime staff felt passed over, often due to a lack of qualifications, and they directed their frustration at incoming administrators. For Joy, it was like stepping onto a battlefield in a war she didn't start and wanted no part of. Fabricated accusations and constant investigations became her new reality, each one designed to break her spirit.

But Joy didn't break. She endured the stress, the sleepless nights, and the responsibility of being the primary provider for her household. When Bleaks Creek finally promoted an HR director from within, Joy thought things might improve. She was wrong.

The best news of Joy's life came one late spring morning. After years of trying, Joy was finally pregnant. She shared the news with HR, expecting congratulations. Instead, she was met with resistance. "You can't just take time off," they said. "Do you know what kind of strain that puts on us?"

Regardless of their improper pleas, Joy exercised her rights to be there for her newborn daughter. She took her maternity leave, determined to put her family first. But when she returned, HR made their hostility clear. The investigations resumed, each one more ridiculous than the last. It felt widespread now, an attempt to push her out by everyone.

That's when she happened to reach out to Margaret Sanders of the Mountain View REB. Margaret's reputation was legendary. Her compliance numbers were the envy of the state. Joy wanted to know her secret.

To her surprise, Margaret had more than advice to offer. "I'm retiring soon," Margaret said. "We're looking for someone just like you. Someone who knows what they're doing."

The idea of leaving Bleaks Creek felt like a lifeline. Mountain View wasn't just a more desirable location; it was a chance to rebuild her life. Joy applied, and when she got the job, the relief was overwhelming.

Packing up their lives once again, Joy, David, and their daughter Billie set out for Mountain View. As the miles rolled along, the restraints of the past began to lift, replaced by a cautionary hope. This time, Joy thought, things would be different.

This time, they were sure to finally find a place to call home.

Chapter 24: The Joy of Chaos

From her first day as Director of Specialized Student Care at Mountain View REB, Joy Denison felt the tension between the pristine image the bureau projected and the chaos lurking beneath. She had been drawn to this position by the bureau's stellar compliance numbers, impressed by the way Mountain View seemed to achieve while others struggled to maintain. But now, only days in, she saw the devil in the details.

Many of the OTs were overworked, some drowning in unmanageable caseloads, while others coasted by with half the workload. There was no clear system for tracking services or ensuring compliance. It wasn't just chaotic. It was a liability, a potential time bomb. And for Joy, who believed in accountability, this went against everything she built her career on.

She understood immediately what her role demanded. Fix it, it whispered. For Joy, her work wasn't just a job; it was a commitment to ensure every child received the support they were promised. And with every barrier she encountered, her resolve only strengthened.

She took her concerns directly to Anthony. Seated across from him in his office, Joy laid out the issues: the unbalanced caseloads, the lack of centralized records, the impossibility of ensuring compliance without a solid tracking system. But as she spoke, Anthony's expression didn't shift. He listened, nodded here and there, but seemed more interested in minimizing the problem than addressing it. When he finally spoke, he dismissed the OTs' frustrations as "typical griping" and advised her to "keep things steady."

Joy left his office unsettled but determined. If she couldn't count on Anthony's support, she would find another way. Special education was too critical to be swept under the rug.

Her next stop was Delilah's office. Perhaps, the Director of Ingenuity might have resources or ideas to help streamline processes. Joy entered with a polite smile, interested in making the most of her colleague's unique, if somewhat eccentric, role.

Delilah greeted her with a bright smile and a distracted wave as she sat at her cluttered desk. "Joy! Special education—isn't it a whirlwind? Loving it yet?"

Joy stayed cordial. "I'm glad to be here. But I wanted to talk with you about a project I think could help everyone. The OT caseloads are screwy, and we have no centralized system to track compliance. I was hoping your department could help us develop a framework or tool to consolidate this information."

Delilah's smile wavered for only a second before she replaced it with her usual enthusiastic expression. "Oh, that sounds like a fun challenge!" she said, leaning forward as if ready to dive in. "But, gosh, we're really focused on forward-thinking projects right now. I mean, compliance is great, but isn't that just so...linear?"

Joy blinked, unsure she had heard correctly. "Linear?"

Delilah's eyes sparkled as she waved a dismissive hand. "Absolutely! We don't want to get bogged down by old-school regulations, do we? Let's think about breaking boundaries here. Let's embrace uncertainty and allow room for flexibility. Compliance is a wonderful concept, but who says it can't be... fluid?"

Joy felt a chill run down her spine. Embrace uncertainty? Fluid compliance? Joy had come to fix real, pressing issues, not drown them in abstract buzzwords. Still, she pushed on.

"Delilah, I understand the desire for innovation, but these regulations are legally binding. They aren't optional. Our department needs a reliable tracking system, and I was hoping you might be able to help us with resources."

Delilah kept her smile intact, although her eyes seemed to lose their warmth. "I completely get where you're coming from, Joy. Really, I do. But right now, I'm in the messy middle of so many projects. My bandwidth is stretched. Maybe IT can help?" With that, she turned back to her computer, signaling the end of the conversation.

Joy left Delilah's office as her optimism gave way to steely determination. Delilah's refusal was not an obstacle. It was a reminder of how much work still lay ahead. Joy would press on, with or without support from the so-called Director of Ingenuity. Compliance was her responsibility now, and she would not ignore it.

Her next stop was Alice in IT. If anyone could help, surely it would be her. Joy explained the situation, detailing the state of disarray, the overloaded therapists, and the absence of any centralized system to monitor services. Alice listened with a sympathetic smile, nodding as Joy spoke.

"Believe me, I wish I had better news," Alice said, leaning back in her chair. "But creating a comprehensive system for tracking compliance? That's a five-year project, minimum. We just don't have the infrastructure right now."

"Five years?" Joy repeated, stunned. "We can't afford to let things go that long."

Alice shrugged apologetically. "I get it. But we're stretched thin, and this kind of project takes time, manpower, and funding. Right now, it's not a priority on the bureau's timeline."

Joy thanked Alice, though a feeling of resignation began settling in. The system's failings weren't just inconvenient, they threatened the very students they were meant to protect. And yet, time after time, Joy found herself alone in her fight for accountability.

But the barriers wouldn't stop her.

That evening, at home, Joy shared her frustrations with her husband and stay-at-home dad, David. Her voice was laced with emotion as she described the hurdles and the indifference she had encountered. David listened intently, his brow furrowing as she spoke.

"Why don't you let me take a look?" he finally offered.

Joy's eyebrows shot up. "You?"

"Why not?" he replied, a small smile tugging at his lips. "I know it's complex, but I can pick it up. I am a data analyst after all. I'm at home with Billie most of the day. I can work on it during her naps and on weekends. And hey, it sounds interesting. Plus, it would give me a chance to support you."

Joy's eyes softened, grateful for his offer. David didn't have a background in database work, but his analytical mind and problem-solving skills had always impressed her. However, there was a catch: the bureau's policy prohibited her from hiring family members. David would have to work without compensation.

"Are you sure?" she asked, feeling a flicker of hope.

David shrugged while adoring her with a warm expression. "Let's do it. We'll call it a passion project."

In the following weeks, David dove into the project, teaching himself the intricacies of database design and coding, often poring over manuals late into the night. He approached it with the same care and dedication that Joy poured into her own work, and slowly, the framework began to take shape. When the bureau agreed to provide a consultant to provide quality assurance, it felt like a small victory, a sign that, despite the challenges, progress was possible.

Meanwhile, Joy focused on bridging the gaps within her department. She met with the therapists individually, listening to their struggles and frustrations, validating the strain they felt. Where the bureau's leadership had previously dismissed them, Joy made sure they felt seen, heard, and valued. Her calm yet unyielding presence breathed new life into a team that had felt overlooked and undervalued for too long.

Joy's commitment didn't go unnoticed. Slowly, her team began to trust her, recognizing her as a leader who wouldn't just talk about change but would do the work necessary to make it happen. And as David's database took shape, Joy felt a growing sense of pride. She wasn't just patching the cracks; she was rebuilding the foundation. Finally, she saw a path forward, one where accountability, fairness, and ethics led the way.

Through every setback, every indifferent response, Joy pushed forward, embodying the true meaning of leadership. While others coasted or avoided responsibility, Joy embraced it, believing wholeheartedly in the impact her work could have on the lives of students and employees. She wasn't after power or admiration. Her mission was simple: to make things right.

And as she glanced over the preliminary reports from David's developing database, Joy felt a sense of fulfillment she hadn't experienced before. The system was still in development, but it was a start, a lifeline for her team and a safeguard for the students under her care. Unlike Anthony's hollow gestures or Delilah's empty rhetoric, Joy's work held real meaning.

Joy closed her laptop that evening with a rare sense of peace. She knew the road ahead remained long, that there would be more challenges, more resistance. But for the first time since stepping into a leadership role, she felt certain of one thing: she was exactly where she needed to be.

And with every step she took, Joy revealed herself as a true leader Mountain View needed, the hero her team and students could rely on. She wasn't in it for recognition or praise. She was in it to make a difference, and that alone made her unstoppable.

Chapter 25: The Age of the Chiefs

When COVID-19 crashed into the world, Anthony saw himself as a victim of circumstance. This was a crisis he hadn't caused, yet it disrupted his carefully arranged life with restrictions, protocols, and "safety requirements" that, from his perspective, only served to limit his freedom. The entire ordeal was a colossal inconvenience, and he had no interest in managing it. So, he did what he always did. He leaned on others to do the heavy lifting while he kept his distance.

His first line of defense was Alice. With remote learning taking over, someone needed to wrangle the bureau's entire technological landscape, and Alice had always been dependable. Anthony didn't see the endless hours she poured into converting systems, training staff, and troubleshooting glitches; he just assumed it would all come together, as if by magic. "Alice will handle it," he told himself, brushing off any deeper thought. "She always does." And indeed, she managed to drag the bureau online while Anthony remained in the background, comfortably removed from the chaos.

But the pandemic brought more than just tech headaches. New regulations meant an endless stream of policy updates, hours of Zoom meetings, and a daily parade of government advisories. This was where Delilah came in handy. She had a knack for looking busy without being effective, and Anthony found her enthusiasm for being in the spotlight useful. He began nudging her to represent the bureau, imagining her friendly nods filling the screens of bureaucrats and officials. The idea was simple: let Delilah handle the public face of the crisis while he stayed out of the limelight.

This arrangement gave Anthony the time and space to focus on something far more important to him: his ambitions. With the notion of "Chiefs" floating in his mind, Anthony began drafting a vision for an "inner circle" he could lead. Delilah's flattery had planted a seed. She called him a "big-dick CEO" offhandedly, and he couldn't shake the idea. It wasn't enough to be Commissioner; he wanted the stature, the title, the respect that came with being a true CEO. And a CEO needed Chiefs.

For months, he'd been crafting the concept in his mind, fantasizing about his team of top executives. Alice would, of course, be Chief of IT; she was indispensable, a worker bee who would keep the wheels turning. Delilah could be Chief of Ingenuity. She praised him, showed loyalty, and knew how to charm others. These were traits he valued far more than qualifications. Joy, however, posed a problem. She managed the bureau's largest department, but she didn't flatter him, didn't play into his vision of authority. Her expertise was unquestionable, but in his world, competence wasn't enough; flattery was the currency that secured power. Joy hadn't invested in him, so she didn't belong in his inner circle.

As he tinkered with this imaginary cabinet of Chiefs, the real-world pandemic raged on, forcing the bureau to adapt to new demands. But Anthony's thoughts were elsewhere. His weekly Zoom trivia sessions became the high point of his week. Since his usual trivia-nights had been canceled due to isolation protocols, he demanded Alice set up virtual trivia for him. It didn't matter that Alice was already spread thin, juggling a relentless stream of tech issues and staff requests. Anthony missed showing off his trivia prowess and felt entitled to it. "Alice can handle it," he thought dismissively, ignoring the visible strain on her face every time she had to schedule yet another call. His ego needed the fix, and Alice's fatigue was a small price to pay.

Meanwhile, with Anthony distracted by his imaginary power circle and Delilah left as the de facto point person, eccentric ideas began entering the mainstream. Employees who had always hovered on the fringes of sanity now found an eager listener in Delilah, who, in her quest for "innovation," started entertaining proposals that bordered on the absurd.

Gene, the Occupational Therapist known for his eccentricity, requested a meeting with Delilah to pitch his latest brainchild.

"Proximity collars!" he announced, eyes gleaming with excitement. "These collars keep people six feet apart. Perfect for classrooms! If kids get too close, they'll get a little buzz. Just a gentle reminder to keep their distance."

Delilah's face lit up. The idea was bizarre, yes, but something about its novelty appealed to her. She pictured herself lauded as the brains behind a groundbreaking new safety measure, maybe even making the news. "Proximity collars," she murmured, testing the words out loud. Genius, she thought. This was her chance to prove she was more than just Anthony's sidekick; she could bring something revolutionary to the table.

Still, Delilah had enough sense to know that special education required a certain finesse, so she decided to run the idea by Joy.

Joy's reaction was swift and unequivocal. "You want to put shock collars on kids?" she asked, her tone barely concealing her disbelief.

Delilah shrugged, brushing off the critique. "Not shock collars, exactly. Just a little buzz. Like a tap on the shoulder. It would keep them from getting too close to each other."

Joy took a deep breath, steadying herself. "Delilah, children don't sit still. They're constantly moving, bumping, running, clustering. Imagine a room full of kids wearing these collars. The moment one kid moves, the whole room would be buzzing. You'd have children jolting and jumping like a human pinball machine, setting each other off all day long."

Delilah tilted her head, clearly not grasping the full implications. "But wouldn't that teach them discipline? If they get buzzed enough, they'll learn."

Joy stared, half-wondering if Delilah was joking. "Delilah, they're children, not animals. We don't train them with shock collars for a reason. Imagine the lawsuits, the emotional trauma, the chaos. The kids who sit still would end up punished by the ones who can't.

And what if a collar malfunctions? A child gets repeatedly buzzed for no reason? Or one kid's collar shocks harder than the others? This isn't a solution. It's a disaster."

Delilah's smile faltered for a second, but she quickly regained it, dismissing Joy's concerns. "Maybe it just needs some refinement. I'll talk to Gene. We'll work out the kinks."

After the call ended, Joy leaned back in her chair, a deep unease settling over her. She hadn't been in the bureau long enough to understand how Delilah had risen so high, but the incompetence was clear. If this was the kind of leadership Anthony valued, then it was going to be a long, exhausting road.

Meanwhile, Anthony sat in his home office, lost in thoughts of grandeur. His concept of Chiefs was taking shape, and soon he believed he would have his team, a cadre of loyalists who would make him appear visionary. He pictured himself one day passing the torch to Delilah, a thought that filled him with satisfaction. She might lack qualifications, but she had loyalty, charm, and, most importantly, she made him feel important.

In Anthony's mind, everything was running smoothly. Alice was handling the tech, Delilah was keeping up appearances, and Joy... well, Joy was there, somewhere. The bureau seemed fine, and as far as he was concerned, he had done his part. Nothing had collapsed yet, and that was proof enough that his plan was working.

With the weekend approaching, Anthony didn't have to pack his bags. He was already enjoying an extended quiet retreat at his lakefront vacation home. There, he only had to deal with occasional Zoom calls and pandemic briefings. He could sit back, relax, and let the world sort itself out.

In his absence, others would handle the mess. And if things unraveled, well, that wasn't his problem. He was going to enjoy his extended vacation... his semi-retirement. This 'woke' medical emergency overreaction wasn't going to dictate his days. Afterall, he wasn't meant to be a part of the working class, he was enjoying the life he was supposed to live, and he dreaded the upcoming in-person daily grind.

Chapter 26: Maddy

The return to in-person work, after the long isolation of COVID protocols, filled the halls of Mountain View REB with a buzz. Faces that had been confined to tiny squares on screens reappeared in full form, their smiles half-familiar, their interactions hesitant but genuine. The energy was a strange, uneasy mix of cautious optimism and the lingering, stringent guidelines they had endured.

For Matt, the Director of Inclusive Services, the return to in-person work felt like a double-edged sword. He had always been well-liked, a steady presence who listened more than he spoke and treated everyone with quiet respect. But the truth was, Matt had spent the months of isolation wrestling with a part of himself he could no longer ignore. Returning to work meant facing people as the version of himself they had always known, but that version felt increasingly like a stranger.

Every interaction became a performance, every smile a mask. The dissonance he lived with his entire life had grown unbearable, and the facades he carefully built to hide it were starting to crumble. Matt didn't want to be Matt anymore. He wanted to be Maddy.

The first person he confided in was Joy. She was the obvious choice. Joy had an uncanny ability to make people feel celebrated for who they are. She was the kind of leader who asked how you were, then genuinely wanted to know the answer. Ever since Joy joined the bureau, Matt had gravitated toward her, sensing her to be a safe and trustworthy friend, a quiet strength that was all too rare.

One late Friday afternoon, the two of them sat across from each other in Joy's office. Matt was fidgeting with his pen, tapping it against the desk in a rhythm Joy recognized as hesitation. She didn't press him nor fill the silence with reassurances or questions. She simply waited, her eyes on the report they were crafting, her presence unshakable.

Finally, Matt spoke. "Joy," he nearly whispered, "can I tell you something? Something I haven't told anyone?"

Joy leaned in, with her typical soft but serious expression. "Of course. Whatever it is, I'm here."

He hesitated then exhaled, the possible consequences of his next words visible in his body language. "I've been thinking about transitioning. About becoming Maddy."

For a moment, the room felt impossibly still. Then Joy smiled. It wasn't the kind of smile people plaster on to feign understanding, but a warm, genuine expression that wrapped around Matt like a blanket. "Thank you for trusting me with this," she said gently. "What does becoming Maddy look like for you?"

Hearing her name uttered by a co-worker for the first time hit Maddy like a jolt of electricity. She began to open up, haltingly at first, then with growing confidence. She told Joy about how she always felt out of place, the moments of clarity that came during the pandemic isolation, and the fears that kept her silent for so long. Joy listened, her presence unwavering, only speaking to ask for clarification or offer encouragement.

When Maddy finished, she looked at Joy with tears in her eyes. "I'm scared," she admitted. "I know some people won't accept me. I don't want to lose my standing."

Joy leaned forward, resting her elbows firmly on the desk, her expression steady yet brimming with quiet intensity. "Maddy, I won't lie to you. Transitioning is going to draw the scorn of some people. The world is full of judgment, and much of it is grossly unfair. But here's some truth: understanding fairness wasn't how I was raised. I had to unlearn so much to be who I am today; others can unlearn too."

Maddy's fear softened a bit, her curiosity flickering to life behind it. Joy offered a wry, almost bittersweet smile, her voice dipping lower, more confessional. "I grew up in a household where being white, straight, and traditional wasn't just expected, it was treated as sacred. My parents didn't preach it outright, but you could hear it in their offhand comments, feel it in their silences, see it in their judgmental glances. I absorbed it all, never questioning how much harm it caused."

She paused, searching for the right words. "Fresh out of college, I worked with this incredible woman, Rochelle. She was sharp, funny, and so kind it was disarming. We became close, and one day, she told me she was gay. It shouldn't have mattered, but it shook me. I went home that night, replaying her words, wondering if I should keep being friends with her. The fact that I even considered ending our friendship over something so personal, so deeply hers, still makes me cringe. I was so caught up in what I'd been taught that I couldn't see how wrong it all was."

Maddy watched Joy closely, her hesitations diminishing under Joy's honest aura. Joy's voice grew more thoughtful, almost wistful. "I've thought a lot about it," she said. "Even when I was little, before I understood anything about relationships or how babies were made, I found myself drawn to boys. And honestly, it didn't make any sense. Boys are loud, dirty, and rough. My friends were all girls. They were the ones I shared secrets and laughter with They're the ones who made me feel welcome. If anything, it would have been logical to be interested in girls. But I wasn't. It just... wasn't how I was wired."

She paused, allowing a reflective smile to bloom. "I can't remember ever choosing who I liked, what music is my jam, or why chocolate is my favorite flavor. I didn't make a list of pros and cons; there wasn't some logical reason behind it. The pull was just there, as natural as breathing. And that's the thing, it's not about deciding who you're drawn to, or weighing qualities like height, or eyes, or voice. Those connections spark from someplace deeper, someplace beyond choice. So how could I ever judge someone else for feeling what's innate to them? Attraction isn't a decision, it's a truth. And it's no one's place to question someone else's truth."

Joy leaned back slightly, her tone growing resolute. "Bigotry against the LGBTQ+ community has so little to do with the target. It's about everyone else projecting their own insecurities, their fears, their need for control onto others. Those arguments about bathrooms, marriage, or competitions? They're not about love or inclusion; they're about using outliers, opportunists or bad actors, as scapegoats to justify systemic cruelty. Sure, there are always a few opportunists who will exploit systems, but that's not unique to any group. Why should an entire community bear the burden of those bad apples? Why should their dignity and happiness be sacrificed because some people can't separate reality from fear?"

She shifted slightly, her gaze locking on Maddy's, her voice softening without losing its strength. "Your identity has no bearing on my life. None. Who you are, how you love, how you present yourself doesn't impact me in any way. But what does matter to me is having coworkers and friends who are happy and authentic. People who aren't carrying the crushing weight of pretending to be someone they're not. That weight breaks people, and I can't stand to see that happen. I'd rather work with people who feel free to be themselves than watch them suffer in silence because they think the world won't accept them."

Joy reached across the desk allowing her hand to rest gently on Maddy's. "The people who have a problem with you... that's their baggage. They're consumed with the need to control how others live. It's not about you. It's about them wanting uniformity in how society should look. That's oppression, plain and simple. I won't stand by and let them dictate who gets to be happy, and neither should you. You have every right to be Maddy, to live your truth, to be free."

Tears welled in Maddy's eyes, her lips trembling as she fought to speak. "Thank you, Joy. I... I didn't know how much I needed to hear that."

Joy's smile widened, warmth and certainty radiating from her. "And I didn't know how much I needed to say it. You matter, Maddy. I'm your ally, not just because it's right, but because I believe in you. You're not alone in this, not now, not ever."

In that moment, the trust between the two intensified and their friendship grew. Together, they faced the daunting weight of what lay ahead, not as individuals, but as allies bound by truth and courage.

The plan for Maddy's workplace transition took shape over the next few hours. Together, she and Joy crafted an announcement to send to the staff. It was short and direct, reflecting Maddy's desire to keep things simple: "From this point forward, I will be known as Maddy and will use she/her pronouns. I appreciate your support and respect as I step into this next chapter. Thank you for your continued kindness as we continue to make Mountain View a place where everyone feels valued and included."

The email went out that Friday afternoon, giving staff the weekend to process the news. The responses were as varied as Maddy had anticipated. Many colleagues sent kind messages of support, their words heartfelt and genuine. Others stumbled awkwardly over pronouns or avoided the topic entirely. Delilah was outwardly enthusiastic, praising Maddy in meetings and making a point of using her name and pronouns. But her enthusiasm felt calculated, more about burnishing her progressive image than offering true support.

Anthony's reaction, however, was the most grating. During a leadership meeting, he addressed Maddy directly, his tone a strange mix of self-satisfaction and condescension.

"I just want to say," he began, "that I used 'she' in a conversation about Maddy this morning. And you know what? It wasn't that hard. We can all do this if we try."

The room fell silent. Maddy forced a polite smile. Joy was in disbelief. Anthony's words, meant to showcase his progressiveness, felt patronizing, reducing Maddy's identity to a personal challenge he'd managed to overcome.

Later, behind closed doors, Anthony's true feelings emerged. "I don't get it," he vented to Delilah. "Why does everything have to change? What's wrong with just being how you were born? This whole thing feels… overly dramatic."

Delilah, ever the opportunist, nodded vaguely. "It's a lot for people to adjust to," she said carefully, neither agreeing nor disagreeing.

Anthony leaned back in his chair, his expression darkening as he gazed toward the ceiling, avoiding Delilah's watchful eyes. "I told you about those mobs at board meetings," he muttered with unease. "It's like they've been trained to use any excuse to tear someone apart. They don't listen to reason. They just come with pitchforks. I'm not about to make this bureau their next battleground."

He paused before his tone hardened as fear readied his defenses. "It's not about being against inclusiveness," he continued, almost to himself. "It's about not inviting chaos. You give these people something to latch onto, and it doesn't matter if it's right or wrong, they'll use it to burn the place down. I can't have that on my watch."

Delilah's silence stretched, and Anthony pressed on, as though trying to convince himself as much as her. "What good does it do to stir the pot? Standing up to them is not bravery if all it does is bring chaos. You end up giving them exactly what they want: madness. They thrive on fear, and honestly..." His voice faltered, then dropped to a near whisper. "I don't want to be their target. I don't want to deal with them."

The room grew still as his admission settled between them like a sour taste. Beneath his words lay the bitter truth: Anthony's fear of the mob didn't just silence him, it made him complicit. In his effort to avoid confrontation, he wasn't just stepping aside; he was conceding the moral ground entirely. And deep down, a part of him knew it, and he didn't care. "I wonder if I should start showing *him* the door?" Anthony wondered out loud.

In the weeks that followed, Maddy's courage rippled through the bureau. Some colleagues began asking questions, seeking to understand gender identity more deeply. Others reflected on their own biases, grappling with discomfort in private rather than projecting it outward. And through it all, Maddy stood tall, her confidence growing with each passing day.

For Joy, the lesson was clear: Maddy's happiness and authenticity had no bearing on anyone else's life. Those who made it about themselves gained nothing but the opportunity to hurt someone brave enough to be different. And for Maddy, the journey wasn't just about pronouns or appearances, it was about finally stepping into the light, free from the shadows of fear.

Anthony leaned back in his office chair, tapping his pen against a printed sample report Joy had left for him. The numbers practically glowed on the page, spelling out compliance figures and caseload balances with pinpoint accuracy. It was a marvel of efficiency, more than he had ever achieved as Director of Specialized Student Care.

Under Joy's guidance, the department hummed, its gears well-oiled and spinning cleanly, and that left him uneasy. It wasn't quite jealousy, but it was something close. Her success cast light on everything he had failed to do, and it was brighter than he could comfortably bear.

Before that feeling could grow teeth, Delilah appeared in his doorway, her presence flipped a switch. She strutted through his office as though she owned it, her lips and eyes flirting with every stride. It wasn't just confidence, it was a deliberate performance, finely tuned to meet Anthony's needs. He exhaled and set the report down, basking in the warmth of her attention.

"Looks like Joy's really gone all in on that database," Delilah remarked, her tone light but with a practiced edge. She perched herself on the corner of his desk, crossing her legs as though she belonged there. "It's... impressive, I suppose."

Anthony nodded, though he appeared slightly nauseated with the conversation. "It is, isn't it? The compliance numbers have never been this clear. Honestly, I wish I'd thought of it when I was in her position."

Delilah laughed softly, brushing a strand of hair behind her ear. "Oh, come on, Anthony. You've always been the big-picture guy. Anyone can shuffle numbers around. It's vision that sets you apart."

Anthony smiled faintly, but his eyes drifted back to the report. The conversation wasn't distracting him the way it usually did. His mind had shifted to something bigger, something more final.

"I've been thinking," he said with a measured tone. "About the future. About retiring at the end of the school year. I find myself longing for the independence the pandemic offered."

Delilah's smile didn't falter, but a flicker of unease crossed her face. "Retirement?" she echoed, her voice just as saucy, but now with an edge of caution. "You're serious?"

"I am," Anthony said. He leaned forward, threading his fingers together. "I've done my part here, built something strong, and the board deserves a successor."

Delilah felt an unease she had never felt in his presence, but she kept it together. "Well, it's obvious who that should be, isn't it?" She smiled wider. "You don't need to look far. I'm right here."

Anthony's eyes narrowed slightly, and he let her words hang there for a moment. "That's one option."

Delilah was taken aback. She shifted her posture, angling herself closer. "Anthony, no one understands your vision better than I do. No one could carry it forward the way I can."

"Joy could," he said plainly.

Delilah's carefully constructed composure cracked for a split second. Her eyes fluttered as she searched his face for some hint of jest, but she found none. "Joy?" she said, keeping her voice light, almost amused. "She's... fine. Competent. But she's not leadership material. She doesn't have your charisma, your ability to inspire." But, most importantly to Delilah, Joy didn't trust her nor have any faith in her capacity as an administrator; her position and salary would be on the line.

"She has results," Anthony countered. "The database alone has put Specialized Student Care ahead of the curve. Staff respect her. She's streamlined operations in ways I never managed." He paused, his gaze steady. "She's a logical choice."

Delilah forced herself to laugh, though the sound came out disingenuous. "Anthony, come on. Logic? This isn't about logic. It's about relationships. Loyalty. Legacy. You know that."

Anthony tilted his head and conjured a faint smile. "Loyalty. That's a lovely word."

Goosebumps engulfed Delilah, her instincts interpreting that something had shifted. However, she kept her cool and remained inviting. "What are you thinking?"

Anthony leaned back in his chair, his eyes sharp and predatory. "You want this, don't you?"

"Of course I do," Delilah said with a steady voice despite the accelerating unease. "No one else can do it."

Anthony's smile widened, though it carried no warmth. "Then let's talk about what I want."

Delilah froze as she felt the weight of his invasive and heavy gaze ogling her. "What do you mean?" she asked with a careful and deliberate tone.

"I've earned the right to leave this bureau on my terms," Anthony calmly said, almost conversational. "And I've earned something for myself."

Delilah's pulse hammered in her ears, but she kept her face neutral. "What are you asking for, Anthony?"

He leaned forward, the space between them shrinking until his voice dropped to a near whisper. "I want you to strip for me. Nude. While I jerk-off behind my desk."

The words struck her like a physical blow and her mind scrambled to process what he had just said. "Anthony," she began, her voice measured, "that's..."

"A condition," he interrupted, smooth and unyielding, with the quiet confidence of someone who expected to be obeyed. "If you refuse, I'll recommend Joy to the board. She's the logical choice, after all. Qualified. Respected."

Delilah's fingers clenched in her lap. She forced herself to smile, although it felt sharp and brittle. "We're both married. I can't do this to Cynthia."

Anthony's smile didn't waver. "Leave Cynthia out of this. There won't be any touching. We'll just be acting out our desires without actually cheating. And don't get any ideas about reporting this. By the time anyone investigates, I'll be gone. And you'll be finished here. The only way you keep what you have—what you want—is by agreeing."

Delilah's stomach churned, but she didn't let it show. She put on a welcoming smile, but it was a hard sell. "If that's what you want, Anthony," she said, the words tasting bitter on her tongue, "then... of course." At this moment, she thought about her mother, and the suffering she endured, and how she overcame the odds. This gave her strength to do what she simply had to do... this indignation had a tradeoff too good to pass up.

Anthony leaned back, satisfaction spreading across his face. "Good. Go lock the door, draw the blinds, and show me how much you want me."

Anthony's eyes moved all over her body as he carefully slid his pants down far enough to start playing with himself. He studied Delilah's form, the way the light hit the curve of her breasts and fell softly against her bare skin. "This is paydirt", he said to himself. A beautiful woman wanted him. It wasn't just a fantasy; it was real. She had chosen to be here, to let him see her like this. The moment felt electric, alive, charged with a kind of validation he had spent years chasing.

This wasn't like before. Not like all those other times. He still holds on to the memory of that passed-out Harvard coed slumped in the bushes outside a party. Her golden hair tangled and her lips parted as she breathed heavily in her drunken haze. He crept over to her and pulled her deeper into the bushes, hoping for better cover. He opened her shirt to expose her bare chest then proceeded to masturbate as he groped her unresponsive body. It was more exciting than the porn he had grown accustomed to. After that "date", he would regularly case the party neighborhoods for other opportunities.

And then there were the countless nights at the bar, where his stockpile of roofies would be dropped into the drinks of unsuspecting travelers just passing through. They were easy marks who would wake up the next day with only questions and no proof.

Those previous "dates", they didn't know him, didn't see him, but that didn't matter anymore. This was different. Delilah wasn't passed out, drugged, or unaware. She was here, awake, fully conscious of what he saw in her. She had chosen to give him this moment, to be his muse. He felt a rush of something powerful, something intoxicating. It was special. It was perfect.

After Anthony finished, Delilah dressed slowly, smoothing her clothes with deliberate care. "That was so exciting, I can't wait to do it again" she said in her playful way.

She calmly walked to the door with measured steps. But as the door clicked shut behind her, the mask fell. Her chest heaved, and her nails dug into her palms. The bile in her throat threatened to rise, but she swallowed it down. Anthony was right, her lifestyle, her career, her very survival depended on pleasing him, but she would never forgive him for this. But even more important, she wasn't going to jeopardize this golden opportunity and end up like her mother.

Chapter 28: Lilith's Burden

Lilith Walker had been the golden child of a family that prized appearances above all else. Her parents paraded her around their small town as a beacon of virtue. Their pride reflected in every stiff nod of approval. She worked in the family's bakery, carried a respectable grade point average as a part-time student at the local community college, and sat in the front pew at church every Sunday. But for all her obedience, she had always felt suffocated under the weight of their expectations, like a doll trapped in a glass case.

That fragile glass shattered one night.

The bar had been loud, filled with laughter and the clink of glasses, and for once, Lilith went on the town and let her hair down. A friend convinced her to go, to step away from her carefully controlled life for a single evening. She found herself drawn to a man at the jukebox. His hat was tilted rakishly, and his ponytail marketed him as not someone she would meet on Sundays. His conversation had wrapped around her like a song. They talked for a while, about what she could no longer remember, but his attention made her feel recognized as the person she might have been if she hadn't lived such a pious life.

The next morning, in her bed, she woke up disoriented and aching. Her dress was rumpled, her legs sore, her mind blank. She couldn't remember leaving the bar, let alone getting home. The ponytailed man's voice lingered faintly in her memory, but it was so hazy it may as well have been a dream.

Weeks later, her period didn't arrive but she didn't make much of it. This sort of thing could happen from time to time. But, when the next one, and then the next one didn't come, concern necessitated action. By the time she sat at her doctor's office, her worst fear had taken root. She was nearly four months pregnant. An abortion was never an option, her upbringing insisted on that. It would be a sin. The man with the ponytail was the only one with answers, but she didn't know anything about him nor how to contact him. She couldn't explain how or why it had happened. She only knew it did.

Her parents didn't bother to hide their disgust.

"A man you don't know and can't remember that you met at a bar?" her father barked with a razor-sharp voice. "Do you hear how whorish that sounds? Where are your morals?"

Her mother's silence cut even deeper. She righteously sat erect in her chair; her lips pressed so tightly together they looked bloodless. The judgment in her eyes burned like acid.

Lilith's words tumbled out in a rush. "I don't remember anything. The last person I remember talking to might know. I think... I think something happened that night. I didn't choose or want this!"

Her father slammed his hand on the table, making her flinch. "Stop lying! You're no better than the other fornicators. You've embarrassed this family, and we won't stand for it."

Her mother stood with her back to her. "You need to leave," she said softly, as if even acknowledging Lilith's existence was a charity.

Just like that, Lilith's life unraveled. Her parents turned her out. Their cold stares escorted her out the door like a curse. She left their house with nothing but the clothes she stuffed in a bag, meager savings, and a crushing weight of shame.

"How did it end up like this?" She asked herself. "A crime was committed against me, but I'm the only one paying a price." If she had chosen to have an abortion, instead of seeking help from her parents, the slate would have been wiped clean and no one would have known any different. But she chose to follow the light, trusting the very people shunning her because of that choice... because someone forced this pregnancy on her.

For months, Lilith struggled against a world that seemed bent on punishing her. She was relegated to cleaning motel rooms and donating plasma. She spent sleepless nights wondering if she'd have enough money for rent. The stigma of her pregnancy followed her everywhere; an unspoken condemnation etched into the faces of strangers and people she once knew. She caught their judgmental glances, their whispered remarks about "girls like her."

Delilah came into the world on a rainy November morning, her tiny cries filling the sterile hospital room. Lilith held her daughter close, tears streaming down her face. Delilah's innocence, her pure, fragile existence, gave Lilith something she hadn't felt in months: purpose. But purpose didn't pay the bills.

When the money ran out, Lilith turned to the only work that paid the rent and kept the utilities going. The neon glow of strip club lights painted her in garish colors, the music pounding in her ears as she danced for men who didn't bother to hide their ogling. She hated every second of it. The way they looked at her, the way her dignity seemed to slip further away with each night. But when she came home to Delilah's tiny sleeping form, she told herself it was worth it.

Delilah grew up in the margins of her mother's life. She learned early how to make peanut butter sandwiches and heat up instant noodles. The TV was her regular companion on nights when Lilith worked late. At school, she was the girl no one wanted to sit next to, her thrift-store clothes and loud personality making her a target for both teachers and classmates.

Holidays were worse. On the rare occasions Lilith took Delilah to her parents' home, the disapproval was palpable. Her family treated Delilah's cousins like royalty, showering them with affection and gifts, while Delilah received little more than polite smiles. She spent those gatherings clinging to her mother, watching from the sidelines as her cousins tore into brightly wrapped presents. Even as a child, she understood that she and her mother were outsiders and not truly a part of the family.

Through sheer defiance, Delilah graduated high school. She wasn't celebrated. There were no parties, no proud relatives in the crowd. She left the ceremony determined to build a life that didn't echo her mother's struggles.

Her beauty became her armor. She worked tirelessly to maintain it, sculpting her body into a vision that turned heads wherever she went. For Delilah, beauty wasn't vanity, it was her only asset. She wanted to find someone who could shield her from the only life she had known.

With great fortune, she met Carl Annette. He seemed like the answer to all her prayers. He was suave, charming, and endlessly confident. Even more, Carl didn't just see her beauty, he admired her ambition. He swept her off her feet with grand gestures and clever quips, but it was his advice that truly captivated her.

"Do you know why I'm successful?" Carl asked rhetorically. "I understand that people don't buy things," Carl continued. "They buy you. Make them feel special, like they need you, and they'll give you anything."

Delilah soaked up his words, seeing in Carl not just a partner but a mentor. Six months after they met, he proposed, and she jumped at the offer.

Marriage brought stability, but it also brought questions. As they lounged on the couch one evening, Carl broached the topic that Delilah had been avoiding.

"I've been thinking," he said, his tone matching the mood. "What do you think about having kids?"

Delilah froze then sat up straight. She covered her face with her hands then looked back at Carl. "I don't want kids," she said firmly.

Carl frowned. "Why not? Kids are great."

Delilah shook her head as she clapped back. "I grew up watching my mother struggle every single day. She gave up everything for me. I don't want that. I don't want to be tied down, and I don't want to warp my body just to raise someone who might resent me."

Carl leaned closer, acknowledging the sensitivity of the topic. "Not every parent feels like that. You'd be an amazing mom, Delilah. I really believe that."

Her voice hardened. "You didn't live my life, Carl. You don't know what it's like to feel like a burden every day. I won't do that to myself, or to a child."

The room fell silent. Carl finally sighed, running a hand through his hair. "Okay," he said. "But how about this, try working at a daycare. See how it feels. If it still doesn't feel right, I'll drop it."

Delilah stared at him, weighing his words. Finally, she nodded. "Fine. I'll try it. But don't expect me to change my mind."

That's how Delilah found herself at Little Horizons Child Care, stepping into a world she wasn't sure she wanted, carrying the weight of the past she couldn't quite escape. It's also where she met her father, who offered her a high paying job.

Anthony had indeed slipped a roofie in Lilith's cocktail that evening by the jukebox. Once it took effect, he whisked her out of the bar and into his car undetected. He fumbled through her purse to find her apartment address and keys. From there, he took her home and had his way with her. He was rarely this successful. This was one of his favorites. It had been so long, and it was so exciting, that he produced just enough sperm to find her egg at the opportune time. While the timing contrasted with Lilith's will, it turned out to be the perfect timing for Anthony to impregnate a woman against all odds... then lust after his own offspring when she matured.

Chapter 29: The Rise of Delilah

Richard Coleman's retirement as the bureau's Affiliation Director came at an opportune time, aligning with Anthony's grand vision of reshaping the bureau under his banner. To most, Richard's departure was just a natural transition, but to Anthony, it was a prime chance to reinforce his inner circle. Delilah Annette, charming, loyal, and ever adept at making Anthony feel like a titan, was the obvious choice.

The announcement came at the next staff meeting. Standing at the podium, Anthony delivered the news with an air of triumph.

"With the upcoming retirement of Richard Coleman, I'm thrilled to announce that Delilah will be stepping into an expanded role as Chief of Affiliation and Ingenuity," he proclaimed. He beamed, reveling in his vision, his "masterstroke" for the future of the bureau.

There was polite applause, but it barely masked the confusion rippling through the room. A few administrators exchanged puzzled glances, eyebrows raised. Chief of Affiliation and Ingenuity? The title felt strange, overblown, like something lifted from a tech company rather than a regional education bureau. And Delilah, who had rarely shown any substance beyond charisma, was a baffling choice for such a impactful role.

At the back of the room, Joy Denison felt the spectacle of cronyism settle over her. She watched, barely containing her disbelief, as Anthony praised Delilah's "innovative leadership." She knew the truth: Delilah had fumbled every project, produced little of value, and was now being rewarded for reasons that had nothing to do with performance.

For Joy, this felt personal. She had led Specialized Student Care with integrity and skill, shouldering immense responsibilities, tackling obstacles Anthony hadn't even acknowledged. Now, here she was, watching someone who barely understood her own role rise through the ranks on nothing but charm. Joy had dedicated herself to making a real difference for her students and her team, yet it was Delilah, with her superficial appeal, who was being handed another title.

As the meeting ended, Joy found herself lingering, observing Delilah bask in the limelight as Anthony offered his enthusiastic congratulations. She could see how completely Delilah had captivated him, and it was both astonishing and infuriating. Anthony once had her full trust. But this? This was pure indulgence.

Joy felt a pulse of frustration, but it wasn't bitterness that lingered. It was something deeper, a renewed sense of purpose. The blatant and meritless favoritism was disappointing to see, but she had a staff to support, and their needs took a front seat.

Meanwhile, Anthony and Delilah retreated to his office, sharing what they saw as a victorious moment.

Delilah leaned against his desk, a gleam in her eye. "Chief of Affiliation and Ingenuity," she murmured, rolling the title off her tongue with satisfaction. "It's so... forward-thinking, don't you think? Exactly the kind of leadership this bureau needs."

Anthony grinned, thrilled by the sound of it. He basked in the feeling of control, of having his most loyal ally in such a pivotal role. "We're changing the bureau," he said, leaning back in his chair. "Together, we're going to leave a legacy that people will remember."

Delilah flashed him with a warm smile, but beneath it, her mind wandered. She knew the reality: her promotion had come easily, too easily. She could charm Anthony, yes, but the board might question her ascension. And with Joy quietly gaining a reputation, Delilah felt insecure.

Her thoughts turned to Joy's database project, that damned database, which was creating a buzz throughout the bureau. Joy had approached her for help first, and she'd dismissed it. Now, it threatened to undermine her standing.

Delilah took a breath, maintaining her placid smile as she leaned closer to Anthony. "You know," she began, in her most manipulative voice, "I've been thinking... Joy is certainly talented, but she seems...disinterested in the status quo."

Anthony's grin faded slightly, and she watched him, seeing the hint of doubt spark in his eyes. He nodded slowly, considering her words.

"I've been noticing that too," he admitted, trying to conceal the slight discomfort that Delilah's observation stirred within him. He's long observed Joy's growing success, her rising influence, and it unsettled him more than he cared to admit. She had been hired as a team player, but somehow, she seemed to be carving out something more dominant.

Delilah continued, her voice calm but deliberate. "She acts like someone with ambitions, Anthony. Ambitions that... well, may not include our vision."

Anthony's brow furrowed, and Delilah saw the opportunity to solidify her hold. She leaned forward, touching his hand lightly.

"Just something to keep an eye on," she said, ever so smoothly. "We must protect our vision for the bureau. And I'm here to help you do that."

Anthony's discomfort faded, replaced by a deep sense of gratitude. He looked at Delilah and saw more than a colleague. She was a partner, someone who truly understood him and stood by him without hesitation. Chief of Affiliation and Ingenuity. The title sounded better each time he thought about it, and this was only the beginning.

"Thank you, Delilah," he said, as his soul filled with admiration. "With you by my side, I feel like we can handle anything... even a pesky rising star like Joy."

Delilah gave him a reassuring smile, already plotting her next move. She would maintain Anthony's favor, watch for Joy's every achievement, and ensure that nothing threatened her carefully crafted rise.

Chapter 30: The CARE Standoff

After nearly a year and a half of painstaking work, CARE, the Comprehensive Access to Records for Education, was no longer in trial mode; it was available for all Mountain View REB employees to use. Joy couldn't help but feel a surge of pride as she watched the bureau's specialists navigate the new system. She had poured so much into this project. What had started as a rudimentary database, had grown into a revolutionary tool. With David's tireless work behind the scenes, CARE had transformed into a streamlined, intuitive system that not only organized notes but brought the department into full compliance, something no one had ever actually achieved.

For the first time, the Specialized Student Care Department was running seamlessly, meeting every mandate, and exceeding state and federal expectations. Compliance, that elusive goal that had plagued the department for years, was now simplified. Specialists throughout the bureau praised the ease and clarity CARE brought to their work, even calling it a "lifesaver."

One of the first to speak up was Alice, the bureau's notoriously critical CIO. "Joy," she said, stopping her in the hallway, "you've set a new standard with CARE. I've never seen anything like it. Your work here is phenomenal."

The praise only multiplied, and with every appreciative word, Joy's heart swelled. CARE represented not just a new tool, but a new era for the department. The compliance numbers were already soaring, specialists were more organized than ever, and the funding the bureau relied upon was now secure. At last, she thought, the bureau had something to celebrate, something that would impact lives.

It didn't take long for other bureaus, across the state, to inquire about licensing CARE. Joy's excitement grew. She saw it as a chance to impact far beyond her bureau. This wasn't just her success; it was a step toward redefining special education for the whole state, and she believed it would be something Anthony would finally value.

She knew she had to tell Anthony. This was a breakthrough for Specialized Student Care and the bureau as a whole. She imagined him listening intently, nodding as he recognized the gravity of what they'd accomplished. This was, in her mind, the culmination of her work here, the moment she could finally show Anthony, and herself, that she was bringing meaningful change and value to the bureau.

When she entered Anthony's office, she found him seated at his desk, leafing through paperwork with a distracted air. Still, she couldn't contain her excitement.

"Anthony," she began, smiling, "CARE is live, and it's already making a difference. Specialists are over the moon about it. They're saying it's the best tool they've ever had."

Anthony barely looked up, his gaze shifting back to his papers with a dismissive air. "That's... nice," he muttered, not bothering to mask his indifference.

"Anthony, it's incredible news," Joy continued, her smile wide with excitement. "The other bureaus are inquiring about licensing CARE. They hear how well it's working for us, and they're willing to pay for access. This could be huge for us, both financially and in terms of our reputation."

He waved a hand dismissively. "Yeah, I'll look into it," he muttered curtly.

Joy felt a pang of disappointment, her enthusiasm deflating as his response settled in. She had expected pride, or at least acknowledgment of the achievement. This tool wasn't just some improvement; it was a crowning achievement for the department and the bureau. CARE ensured compliance, secured funding, and elevated the bureau's reputation. How could he not see that?

"Anthony," she pressed with a voice laced with disbelief, "this system isn't just a win for the department. It's a huge step for the entire bureau. CARE is something we can take pride in. I thought you'd be... well, thrilled."

Joy stood in silence, watching him shuffle papers, feeling a strange oppression shoving her towards the door. She had poured herself into this project, hoping it would not only benefit the bureau but bring a sense of unity and pride. But instead of enthusiasm, she was met with apathy.

While her mind was left reeling, she turned and left. Why had he brushed her off like that? She couldn't shake the feeling that Anthony was downplaying her achievement deliberately, as though he wanted it to disappear into the background.

The truth is, Anthony was seething. CARE represented everything he despised: technology, change, and above all, a success story that had nothing to do with him or an ally. Joy's work hadn't just improved compliance; it had cast a spotlight on years of failures by the Specialized Student Care Department, failures that had happened under his watch. Her project highlighted his own inadequacies, a harsh reminder that the department had run inefficiently until she'd stepped in.

But Joy pressed forward, fueled by a deeper commitment to her work. With Alice's help, she connected with the business and legal teams to prepare contracts for licensing CARE. Specialists from other bureaus could benefit, and for the first time, David's tireless work would bring him well-deserved recognition. Together, they were about to make a difference far beyond Mountain View.

A few days later, there was a knock at Anthony's door.

"Mr. Pollock," a lawyer from his legal department began. "There's an issue with the CARE contracts. We've been reviewing the licensing rights, and we found that David Denison has the best claim of intellectual property over the software. Since he was never compensated by the bureau for its development, CARE likely belongs to him."

Anthony froze, his pen hovering above a stack of papers. "What do you mean?"

The lawyer cleared his throat, "If we move forward without securing the rights from David, we could face legal issues. We would need to compensate him directly or negotiate the rights."

Anthony's irritation flared, a mixture of anger and insecurity twisting in his gut. How had Joy managed to turn this trivial project into an issue for him, and make him look like a fool in the process? He had dismissed CARE, ignored its development, and now it was set to make her a hero while highlighting his failures. Joy had gone from an obedient employee to a rising star, and it made him feel small.

Later that day, Delilah burst into his office, her expression thunderous. "How could you let this happen?" she demanded, slamming her fist on his desk.

Anthony looked up, taken aback. "What are you talking about, Delilah?"

"CARE, that damn database," she snapped. "It's all the other bureaus are talking about! Joy's become the state's golden child overnight. Specialized Student Care Directors are praising her left and right, and the board is bound to hear about it. She's positioned herself as more valuable than the both of us, Anthony!"

Her words hit him like a sucker punch. Delilah was right. The board loved results, and Joy's achievements with CARE were exactly the kind of success story they couldn't resist. If Joy gained enough momentum, she could overshadow Delilah, his chosen successor. The thought stung, adding fuel to his resentment.

"She's already made you look obsolete," Delilah continued, with venomous discontent. "And I'm sure she's planning to replace you and I in the board's eyes. You need to shut this down, Anthony. Now."

Anthony clenched his jaw, feeling Delilah's anger and his own brewing fury. "We can't let her progress," he agreed, his voice cold. "I'll make sure CARE doesn't get any bigger than it already is."

Delilah leaned in, her eyes gleaming with satisfaction. "Good. We can't afford to let Joy steal the spotlight. She's not one of us, Anthony. And she'll use this to undermine everything you've built."

Her words sank in, driving his resentment to a boiling point. He would stop CARE before it became a threat to his power, and hers.

The following morning, Joy entered his office, her face beaming with anticipation. "Anthony, the contracts are ready to go. The other bureaus are just waiting for your approval."

Anthony glared at her, his earlier irritation now a full-blown storm. "No," he snapped.

Joy froze, taken aback. "What do you mean, 'no'?"

"CARE is done," he declared, with conviction. "I don't want this bureau tangled up in licensing software. We're not a tech company, Joy."

"But...Anthony, we're ready. Other bureaus need this, and David's work deserves recognition." Her voice trembled; the weight of his words settled over her like a tidal wave.

Anthony's face darkened. "I don't care how far along it is. We're not risking legal liability over some silly project. This ends now."

Defeated and shaken, Joy left his office, her mind spinning. She had never imagined he would sabotage something so valuable. What liability? We are using it with great success. The liability would be in not using it. Everything she had worked towards, everything David had sacrificed, had just been wiped away because of Anthony behaving irrationally.

When Joy shared Anthony's refusal to move forward with licensing CARE, David sat stunned, his mind caught between disbelief and frustration. "He won't even consider it? Won't even listen?" His voice held a faint, desperate hope, as if Joy might reveal she had misunderstood Anthony's cold dismissal. But Joy's weary expression told him otherwise, her eyes reflecting an exhaustion that mirrored his own.

David shook his head, struggling to comprehend. "Does he even realize how much work went into this? I didn't do this for me. I did it to make things better—for the kids, for the specialists, for you, for the damn bureau!" His words edged with disbelief, as though he were grasping for an explanation that would make Anthony's actions logical. But he knew there was none. "He hasn't even bothered to thank me. Not once."

The reality of it all crushed him. He spent months sacrificing sleep, time, and energy, pouring himself into a project that wasn't just another database. It was his labor of love, crafted with meticulous care, intended to bring order to a chaotic system, for all the right reasons. And Anthony had tossed it aside as though it was nothing. Worse yet, he twisted it into something he could control, stripping David of any credit or reward, leaving him feeling discarded, used.

David gazed into the distance. "I'm a stay-at-home dad, Joy. I'm not set up to run a tech company. I didn't do this to start a business." He paused, swallowing hard. "But if he won't let the bureau license it, then I'll do what I must, I guess. These bureaus need it, and I have every right to claim intellectual property." His voice softened as he looked at her, eyes filled with reluctant resolve. "Not because I want to go down that road, but because it's the right thing to do. CARE was meant to help. I can't let Anthony bury it out of...whatever this is."

Joy nodded, but a shadow of doubt crossed her face. "David, I understand why you feel that way," she said, choosing her words carefully. "But if you go down this path, claiming intellectual property, don't you think that might provoke Anthony? He's not proving to be reasonable about this. It might just...make things worse." Her tone was soft but edged with worry, the words floating between them like a warning.

David shook off her concerns. "I get what you're saying, Joy, but he's already said he's not interested in being a software company, right? He's all but spelled it out." His voice steadied, determination hardening his tone. "This way, he doesn't have to deal with it. He can wash his hands clean. And it gives the other bureaus the solution they need."

Joy sighed, still unconvinced. "You're probably right... but I don't know. I know how he operates now, how he thinks." She cast him a glance, a quiet skepticism coloring her expression. "I just don't see him sitting back and letting this slide, even if it is the natural, elegant solution."

David looked at her, feeling her skepticism but refusing to let it take root. "Maybe he's not reasonable, but it's time he acts like he's a leader, someone who cares about what's best for the people he's supposed to serve," his response was laced with frustration. "I can't let his arrogance destroy something that could help so many people. Claiming IP is the alternative. It's the obvious next step."

Joy squeezed his hand, her gaze meeting him. "Then do it. But just... brace yourself. I don't want you to be blindsided if this goes south."

The resolve in his eyes was unshakable. "I know," he murmured, his fists clenched with a quiet defiance. "I'll write up a claim, and you can hand it off to him. I'll make this right, Joy." His words felt both steady and fragile, as if holding back the grief beneath his determination. He didn't want to take this path, but he couldn't see any other choice.

But beneath his steely resolve, sadness lingered, a deep, weary sadness that gnawed at him. "It's hard to believe," he murmured, more to himself than to Joy, "that someone in his position could be this... callous." He looked away, his gaze distant. "I don't get it, Joy. I just don't."

For a moment, they sat in silence, two people forced to face the brutal reality that the system they had believed in, the people they had trusted, could be so ruthless. And as David finally met Joy's gaze, his weary eyes filled with grit that masked his heartbreak, they both understood that they had crossed a line they could never uncross.

A few days after David claimed intellectual property over CARE, Anthony invited him to his office under the pretense of a friendly discussion on how to work together. He leaned back in his chair, adjusting his tie and straightening his posture, savoring the dark thrill coursing through him. Today, he wouldn't just fire David; he'd crush him, dismantling every inch of the pride and hard work David had poured into CARE. The feeling of power surged through Anthony as he prepared for the confrontation.

When David entered, Anthony greeted him with a smile that was too confident, too mischievous. David's eyes narrowed, sensing misplaced pleasure for something so serious.

"Anthony," David began cautiously. "Thanks for meeting with me. I wanted to clear up some confusion about CARE. I would like nothing more than to partner with the bureau."

Anthony raised a hand, silencing him with a condescending smile. "Oh, David, don't worry. I've reviewed everything with our legal team. I can clear this up for you."

David's heart jumped out of his chest. Anthony's didn't call this meeting towards resolution; he was patronizing and calculated. He felt like a mouse trapped under the cold gaze of a predator.

"I understand you've put a lot of effort into this database, and we appreciate it," Anthony continued, every word oozing with false warmth. "But there's been a bit of a misunderstanding on your part. Technically, the bureau paid you for hours spent training staff to use CARE. Those hours were logged, and that legally makes you an employee. Besides, you didn't fill out the proper paperwork to be a volunteer."

David's spirit pushed back, his voice edged with disbelief. "That's absurd. I volunteered my time to help Joy and the bureau. My intention was to support their work, not to lose my own."

Anthony's smirk only grew as he gestured to a stack of paperwork on his desk. "Intentions aside, the law's the law. Since Joy supervised your work, we're claiming CARE as bureau property." He tapped the termination letter in front of him. "Effective immediately, we're letting you go and claiming intellectual property."

David's eyes flashed with shock and disbelief. "Letting me go? I was never an employee. And Joy didn't supervise me; we collaborated, Anthony. CARE was my creation, my vision."

A gleam of satisfaction flickered in Anthony's eyes. "It's all in the documentation, David. Every training session, every touchpoint with Joy, meticulously documented. You're outmatched. And we have an entire legal team prepared to back this up."

David's heart raced as the reality of Anthony's words sank in. This wasn't a discussion; it was a calculated, ruthless ploy to strip him of everything. The hours of careful coding, the intricate design, all seized in an instant. And with it, a realization dawned, chilling him to the core: if Anthony could crush him so easily, Joy's career was at risk too. If Anthony would betray a man who had only ever helped, there was nothing he wouldn't do to protect his control.

David tamed his fury while it roiled in his core. "This isn't right," he protested. "You're mistreating the people who sacrificed for you, who trusted you."

Anthony's face hardened, all traces of faux friendliness vanishing. "I make decisions here, David. You made something great... and we'll take it from here."

David stared at him, grappling with the crushing finality of it. This man, his wife's superior, someone he just rescued from serious liabilities, was ready to destroy everything for unknown reasons. In that moment, he knew any fight he mounted would put Joy in harm's way.

Anthony's voice dropped to a near whisper, his words dripping with malice. "Consider yourself lucky, David. This could have ended much worse. Now," he gestured toward the door, "we're finished here."

David left, each step feeling heavier, his respect for Anthony shattered. CARE, his work, wasn't his anymore. His wife's career dangled by a thread. Anthony had made his intentions painfully clear: challenging him would be expensive, and Joy would pay.

Inside his office, Anthony reclined in his chair, savoring the surge of triumph. He had secured his control, crushed a potential rival, and shown Delilah the extent of his power. The taste of victory lingered, bitter and sweet, as he relished the memory of David's shattered face.

Later, Delilah sat across from him with a satisfied smile. "You should fire Joy too," she confidently suggested. "She's a threat, Anthony. You know it."

Anthony shook his head, a calculated gleam in his eyes. "I don't need to fire her. I've castrated her. She won't cross us again."

Delilah smiled approvingly. Joy's accomplishments had been silenced, and now, they could proceed without interference. "Now seems like a good time for titties," Delilah beamed. "I even wore my finest lingerie today…"

Meanwhile, for Joy, the devastation ran deep. CARE had been more than just a project; it was her commitment to creating a better, more compliant department. Now, it was out of her hands, and with it, the belief that integrity could triumph in a world ruled by people like Anthony.

But even as she sat beside David, comforting him in their shared heartbreak, a quiet resolve began to form. Anthony had won this battle, but Joy wasn't finished. She would bide her time, waiting for the moment when truth and justice could finally have their day.

Chapter 31: Joy's Comeuppance

For Joy Ames, the world had twisted into a nightmare. As she sat across from David in their quiet living room, recounting his meeting with Anthony, she struggled to grasp the depths of betrayal. She had poured herself into CARE, believing it was about compliance, progress, and empowering educators. But to Anthony, it had never been about that. He belittled the project, brushed it aside, and now was twisting it into success that he'd own.

"It is so bizarre," Joy said, her voice barely above a whisper. She paced the room, still reeling. "He kept saying, 'We're not a software company.' But that was never the point! CARE was about helping others, about setting a standard, not about selling software."

David's eyes darkened as he listened. "This isn't about CARE, Joy. It's clearly about something else. Something hidden from sight and nefarious."

Joy slumped onto the couch beside him, feeling the weight of it all. A man who had everything, title, power, influence, was willing to crush anyone who dared to excel in his presence. Anthony and Delilah didn't just want power; they wanted a monopoly on recognition. And Joy, despite her commitment and integrity, was standing in their way.

That night, as she scanned through her emails, an old message from HR caught her eye. She opened it, and her heart skipped as she reread the words: the email confirmed David's role as an approved volunteer on the CARE project. His volunteer status had been sanctioned. A spark of hope ignited within her.

"Look," she said, showing the email to David. "He's basing his claim that you were an employee. HR approved you as a volunteer. He has to question his legal grounds to claim CARE."

David's face broke into a rare smile. "So, we have proof. He can't just erase us from this project."

The following morning, with renewed confidence, David placed a call to Anthony. "Anthony, we need to talk. I've reviewed an email from HR, and it's clear my role was as a sanctioned volunteer on CARE. Your claim about the bureau owning it is based on me being an employee. According to copyright law, volunteers own the work they produce."

Anthony went silent at the other end, his mind racing. David had challenged him. Rage boiled beneath his calm response. "I'll review it with legal," he muttered, and the line went dead.

After slamming down the phone, Anthony paced his office, fury contorting his face. How dare David stand in his way, this man he barely considered a professional threat? Anthony clenched his fists, his mind swirling with plans to stamp out any semblance of Joy's success. He wouldn't allow her to upstage him, not after all he'd done to mold his vision of the bureau. If it meant annihilating her career, so be it.

He called in Delilah, who arrived promptly, her expression one of cold amusement. She loved nothing more than a good takedown, and the gleam in Anthony's eyes told her this would be no ordinary meeting.

"David's becoming a problem," Anthony growled, his hands clenched in frustration. "He's got documentation from HR that could invalidate our claim over CARE. He's a liability."

Delilah leaned back in her chair, her lips edging into a knowing smile. "There's a way to handle this," she said, her voice laced with poison. "Hire an outside investigator. Make it look legitimate, like you're doing everything by the book, but make sure the investigator understands the conclusion you want."

Anthony's brows lifted, intrigued. An investigator would lend an air of authority, a veneer of due process while quietly dismantling Joy's reputation. "Find me someone ruthless," he ordered.

Days later, Delilah introduced Richard Kincaid, an investigator notorious for his loyalty to clients' wishes. Within hours, a directive was issued to Joy, ordering her to a meeting with Kincaid, offering no explanation and no time to prepare.

The next morning, Joy walked into a dim, windowless room where Kincaid sat, his gaze cool and unyielding. His legal pad rested before him, a thin smirk playing across his face as he sized her up.

"Ms. Denison," he began, "we're here to discuss your involvement with the CARE project."

The questions started innocently enough, but soon they grew sharp and accusatory, designed to trap her. "Did you or your husband intend to profit from CARE?" he demanded, his words laced with insinuation.

Joy's pulse quickened, but she kept her voice steady. "No. CARE was created for compliance. The interest from other bureaus came later."

Kincaid's eyes narrowed. "You expect us to believe that you and your husband invested all that time and effort purely out of goodwill?"

"Yes," Joy replied firmly, refusing to let him manipulate her narrative. "It was always about helping the bureau. Nothing else."

The hours dragged on, Kincaid's questions growing harsher, his tone laced with contempt. He twisted every answer, framing her intentions as greedy and self-serving. But Joy held her ground, refusing to let him distort the truth.

While the investigation dragged on for months, David's disillusionment deepened. Witnessing the lengths Anthony would go to sabotage them filled him with moral discomfort. He set out to create a new system, one more powerful, intuitive, and streamlined than CARE. After all, he'd completed the research and knew exactly how to build a better version, incorporating features CARE's cumbersome framework had struggled to handle. In just two months, he crafted a sleeker replacement, his expertise making the process efficient and purposeful. It wasn't long before another bureau expressed interest in purchasing it, and for the first time in months, hope bloomed again.

But before the ink could dry on an agreement, the purchasing bureau's Commissioner, David Harper, reached out to Anthony. "I wanted to check if there's any conflict with Mountain View before we finalize this," Harper explained.

Anthony's blood boiled. David was trying to outmaneuver him. Again.

"He's infringing on our intellectual property," he boldly claimed. "Any partnership with him will result in legal action."

Harper immediately backed down, unwilling to entangle his bureau in a lawsuit. The deal evaporated in an instant, stranding David on an island separated from earnings by Anthony's rough seas.

Anthony's satisfaction quickly soured when his legal team warned him that his baseless threat had crossed a line, exposing the bureau to potential liability for interference. He couldn't let the news leak to Joy. Now, her mere presence was a liability. He needed her gone.

In a closed-door meeting with Delilah and the legal team, Anthony issued his final decree. "I don't care what the investigation finds," he sneered. "Make sure we can fire her. Fabricate findings if you have to."

Delilah's smile widened, triumphant. Joy's downfall would cement her position as Anthony's chosen heir, clearing the path to ultimate control and solidifying her place as the undisputed successor.

Within a week, a doctored report surfaced, painting Joy as a liability, someone who sought to improperly profit from her position within the organization. She was summoned to Anthony's office, where he handed her a termination letter.

"You're done," he said, each word precise and cold. "You'll receive six months' pay if you sign the NDA and disappear quietly."

Joy stared down at the papers, her world unraveling. Everything she and David had built, their sacrifices, the nights of work, they were erasing it all, burying it under deceit.

At home, Joy and David sat at the kitchen table, the day's aggression still whipping through them like the winds of a hurricane. David clenched his fists, fury burning behind his eyes.

"They're destroying us," he muttered. "Not because of CARE, but because they can't bear to let us succeed."

Joy nodded, her voice hoarse with grief. "They're not just taking my job. They're taking our future."

She signed the NDA as it was her best option, barring an expensive and perilous legal fight. The bitter taste of defeat clinging to her tongue, sharp and unrelenting.

But Anthony's vendetta didn't stop there. Determined to erase her from the profession altogether, he filed a baseless complaint against Joy, targeting her educator's license. This wasn't just a petty act of revenge; it was a calculated move to obliterate her prospects entirely. Districts and bureaus rarely hire anyone under investigation, especially in a role as critical as hers. Being under scrutiny implied severe misconduct, the kind that could jeopardize children's welfare and tarnish the district's reputation. For most administrators, a flagged license was a death knell, a mark no amount of explanation could scrub away.

Anthony understood this. He knew that an educator's license investigation, even one lacking any real evidence, could stretch on for years, casting an unshakable shadow over her record. In that time, Joy would remain effectively blacklisted. Her career was in ruin before she even had a chance to defend herself. It wasn't just about sidelining her; it was a total annihilation of her professional identity, a methodical erasure of everything she'd built. By the time the investigation might finally clear her name, no district or bureau would remember her accomplishments. Her reputation, once sterling, would be irreparably tainted, her career quietly, ruthlessly destroyed.

That evening, Anthony and Delilah celebrated in a darkened karaoke bar, their laughter spilling into the night as they reveled in their victory. To them, this was triumph: they had erased Joy, shattered her dreams, and solidified their grip on the bureau.

For Joy and David, it was the end of everything they had worked towards, obliterated by the ruthless ambitions of a man who had placed his ego above justice, and a woman who had secured her place by his side.

Chapter 32: No Regrets

Anthony Pollock leaned back into his leather chair, savoring the way it creaked beneath him, settling into the familiar luxury that only he, the Commissioner, could claim. He had done it. He'd survived the chaos, crushed Joy Ames, and dismantled David's foolish challenges. The world had realigned itself under his command, just as it should. He took in the silent, sterile office around him, the lingering aura of respect, the faint echo of awe that followed him. He felt untouchable.

At his desk, he envisioned a framed newspaper clipping winking at him: "CARE: A Revolution for Specialized Student Care." Anthony would relish such an article. It would attribute CARE's transformative power solely to Mountain View without a whisper of Joy's or David's names. He'd ensured that. His father had always taught him that legacy was not about truth but control. The spoils belonged to the one with the power to seize them, and Anthony had done exactly that. Before the board, he credited CARE's success to Delilah, anointing her as the department's "visionary." No one dared to question him openly, though he'd caught more than one skeptical glance. Let them wonder, he thought. His father would have approved of his ambition, of this meticulous ownership over the narrative.

Delilah soaked up the praise. Her coy smile and thanks were like syrup that she poured onto his ego. He molded her, lifted her, and now she reflected back the admiration he craved. She was his creation, his waste of resources, his demonstration of loyalty rewarded. She leaned close to him after the board meeting, her blouse casually loose, whispering words crafted just for him. "Anthony, you're more than a Commissioner," she'd purred, her voice dropping low. "You're my big-dick CEO. No one else could have done what you've done. This next striptease will be the best yet."

He had basked in her flattery, letting it feed the pride he felt, that particular thrill he knew his father would have appreciated. It didn't matter that none of it was true—that CARE was Joy's vision and David had crafted it from scratch. CARE belonged to him now, and he would twist its legacy any way he pleased. As for Delilah, she existed in his life because he shaped her into the perfect acolyte, a figurehead he controlled. She was everything his father had encouraged him to cultivate: disposable yet useful, charismatic but vacant, a figure to flaunt when others sought the leader behind the curtain, a trophy.

But as Anthony's retirement approached, so too did the faults in his empire. Joy's absence left a void that no amount of Delilah's empty charms could fill. Joy had held the department together, her leadership was a steady force that had kept chaos at bay. Without her, the specialists grew disgruntled, murmuring among themselves, as bitterness simmered. People noticed that the credit for CARE had gone to Delilah—a figure they saw as vapid, a decoration more than a leader. And they noticed that Joy, the department's bedrock, had been vanished. Anthony didn't bother to acknowledge these shifts; his time at the bureau was drawing to a close, and he cared only about preserving his image, not the truth beneath it.

Still, he couldn't shake the unease that gnawed at him. He'd spent years rising through these ranks, controlling every narrative, believing he'd built something unassailable. But as he announced his retirement, the board blindsided him with resistance. They agreed to his departure but insisted on opening the Commissioner position to a full search. They refused to let him hand the role to Delilah.

Anthony's irritation flared. "Why do we need to open it up?" he asked, trying to mask his anger. "Delilah has been groomed for this position. She's ready."

Madalyn Greene, a shrewd board member with no patience for his antics, leaned forward with a cold and unwavering gaze. "Anthony, the next Commissioner needs experience in schools, not just a talent for management," she said. "It's not enough to promote someone based on... other qualities."

Her words struck like a left jab, each one laced with barely veiled reproach. In that moment, he realized they would never allow Delilah to take his place. To the board, she was a farce, a placeholder in an elaborate performance choreographed entirely by Anthony.

He was spinning. Frustration mingled with bitter pride. Madalyn's words stung, and he didn't understand. His ruthlessness and manipulation had been the lessons his father taught him from the beginning. Barton would have nodded with approval, seeing that his son had used people like tools, discarded them once dull, and preserved the legacy of power at all costs. So why was this board member stepping out of line? Why was she questioning something that had always been the plan?

When the interviews began, Delilah tried her best to dazzle the board, casting her lack of experience as an asset, a "fresh perspective." But Madalyn saw through the performance and shut down Delilah's ambitions with precision, leaving no doubt that the board sought genuine experience.

Delilah stormed into Anthony's office the day she learned the news, fury radiating off her. She slammed the door behind her and marched forward, her heels striking the floor like hammers. "You promised me this job," she hissed, venom in every word. "You said I'd be the next Commissioner!"

Anthony raised his hands, trying to deflect her rage. "Delilah, I did what I could. The board…"

"The board?" she sneered while her eyes narrowed. "You've always controlled the board. This is on you. You failed me."

Gone was the doting, flattering Delilah. In her place stood a woman who had used him, wielding her ambition like a weapon. Anthony saw, perhaps for the first time, the full scope of her contempt, and the sting of her scorn.

"You disgust me," she said, leaning closer, her face contorted with disdain. "Did you think I was interested in you? You and your little pecker?" Her voice dropped to a scornful whisper. "I know you're small, Anthony. I wouldn't touch you with a ten-foot pole. I used you. And you failed me."

Her words cut deep, stripping him bare, exposing the frail core of his pride. He had let himself believe her praise, let himself imagine she felt the admiration she so skillfully wielded. But it had all been a sham, an illusion spun with his own ego as the thread. He watched, stunned, as she turned on her heel and stormed out, leaving him alone.

Delilah faded into obscurity soon after, accepting a consulting job where she could peddle her buzzwords and hollow promises. And as she disappeared from the bureau's history, so too did Anthony's power. He retired quietly, no longer the ruler of his once-great empire but an aging man who had burned too many bridges.

In the quiet solitude of his home, he faced the emptiness he'd crafted. His phone remained silent, the people who once fawned over him now distant, and he found himself alone, with only the echo of his father's voice in his mind.

But in the silence, Anthony felt a strange satisfaction. Joy and David were crushed beneath his ambition. Delilah was used and discarded. And the bureau, shaped by his vision, was forever altered by his will. He'd done it. He carried on his father's legacy. He embraced Barton's teachings, made ruthlessness his mark, wielded power as the only truth.

In his darkest thoughts, he smiled. Barton would be proud. His son had learned to use loyalty as a tool, compassion as a weakness, and manipulation as the highest form of survival. He had always been selfish, always been calculating. He took what he wanted by any means necessary, and that was what made him a Pollock. He was no underdog. He was something greater, something his father would have called a true victor. He felt no regret. This was who he was, and he wouldn't have it any other way.

Afterword

In today's world, opportunists have found new strength. They flood our screens, our airwaves, and political halls, pushing messages that might sound comforting, even empowering, but are drenched in manipulation. These voices belong to those who serve only their own interests, convincing followers to turn against family, neighbors, and the vulnerable. They use fear and flattery as tools, aiming to divide us to serve their own ambitions.

Flattery can be a tempting escape, making you feel essential, as though you're on the right side of things. But when it mingles with prejudice, asking you to demonize those who differ or disagree, it becomes a trap set by those who thrive on chaos, control, and exploitation.

Consider the price of following these manipulators. They retreat to places you'll never reach, communities built on the backs of those who trust them blindly. They don't work for you. They use you to construct a system that serves them alone, a world where their power goes unchallenged as the rest of us grapple with the divisions they've created.

So, when someone calls on you to turn against your family, your friends, your community, recognize what they're asking: they want you to turn against yourself. They demand you betray the very people who stand by you, the values that bind us. And for what, a hollow promise or a tax cut that costs more in integrity than it's worth?

Refuse to do their bidding. Avoid their traps. No promise they make is worth the price of your humanity, and the promises they do make are rarely kept. In the end, all they want is to exploit your faith for their gain, leaving you with nothing in return. They will not share their wealth. Whatever we give them, they will use to expand their own share while shrinking ours.

Choose wisely. Choose compassion over division, integrity over hollow praise, and community over chaos. Above all, trust what they do more than what they say. The future we create depends on it.